"What is it exactly that you do for Beaux Hommes, Mr. Walsh?"

His eyes grew hooded. Tossing his glasses onto the desk behind him, he slowly pulled his sweatshirt off to reveal a wickedly cut torso, his obliques so defined they were like funnels for the eye, drawing it straight to... Whoa.

Harper lost her battle to subdue a heated blush. "You're a stripper. Why are you working in the office?"

His face closed down. "They keep the Hooked on Phonics in the closet for us to come by and use whenever we want."

"I didn't mean it that way," she fumbled, beyond irritated that she'd so completely lost her footing. She'd known he was a stripper. She just hadn't expected him to own it with such authority—or to demonstrate it.

His shoulders went rigid. "Stop assuming I'm stupid."

"Then stop using your body as your primary asset!"

And that, right there, was the problem. She'd assumed he was harmless.

She wouldn't make that mistake again.

Dear Reader,

Welcome to the third book set in the world of Beaux Hommes, the most exclusive all-male revue in Seattle. This story definitely showcases some of the hottest skills the men have, not the least of which is brains. The men are all more than fun personalities and, well, *great* bodies. They're all driven to find the ultimate success.

Oh! You're curious about their greatest skills? They might argue, but I'm going to set the record straight: their capacity to love wildly is off the charts.

Writing this, the third book in the trilogy, was the most challenging story I've ever undertaken. Never before have I had two characters so absolutely opposite to each other, two people who have very legitimate reasons to distrust, even dislike, each other from the moment they meet. Our hero has a past that still haunts him and drives him to find monetary success. He's taken on financial responsibility for more than just himself, and he takes his obligations seriously. But there's more at stake for him than the bottom dollar.

And our heroine? So much is going on behind the face she shows every day. Glass ceilings, inner-office politics and a history of heartache have combined to make her who she is—cautious by nature and a definite stickler for rules. Irony twists her into knots when both she and our hero discover she's the one person who can save his future or see him awarded three meals a day and recreation time...in prison.

Pulled Under is a story about being willing to take the kind of chances that force a person to walk the tightrope strung between want and need. Even more, this story is about discovering the confidence to follow one's heart. When it goes against everything a person believes in? That's when a person finds out just how far they're willing to go for the ultimate payout.

Love.

Fondly,

Kelli Ireland

Kelli Ireland

Pulled Under

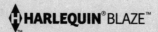

HARLEQUIN® BLAZE™

Recycling programs
for this product may
not exist in your area.

ISBN-13: 978-0-373-79842-1

Pulled Under

Printed in U.S.A.

Kelli Ireland spent a decade as a name on a door in corporate America. Unexpectedly liberated by Fate's sense of humor, she chose to carpe the diem and pursue her passion for writing. A fan of happily-ever-afters, she found she loved being the puppet master for the most unlikely couples. Seeing them through the best and worst of each other while helping them survive the joys and disasters of falling in love? Best. Thing. Ever. Visit Kelli's website at kelliireland.com.

Books by Kelli Ireland

HARLEQUIN BLAZE

Pleasure Before Business
Stripped Down
Wound Up

To Adrienne.

Without you, this story simply wouldn't have been.
I owe you *huge*.

_1_

A PAPER AIRPLANE soared over the top of Harper Banks's cubicle wall and bounced off her computer screen. She picked it up and unfolded it, then scowled. The plane had been made of what had to be the hundredth copy to circulate the office from her most famous pinup photo shoot for a custom motorcycle magazine. Disgust drove a hot flush across her skin.

"Ignore them, Harper." Daniel Miller looked over his shoulder and shouted, "You guys cut the crap already!"

"Forget it, Daniel. They won't stop. I've moved on." A woman might think the universe would cut her a little slack for a slew of bad decisions, but no. No slack for her. She'd spent the past five years paying for blindly leaping for that elusive gold ring—and failing.

Her cell gave a Harley-like rumble, the ringtone she'd set for her dad.

"I need to take this," she muttered, turning to face her desk. She swiped her thumb across the screen and propped the phone between her shoulder and ear so she could talk and type. "Hey, Dad. What's up?"

On the other end of the phone, the TV volume decreased and papers rustled. "How's the IRS's newest senior field investigator managing today?" her dad asked, gravelly voice rumbling from deep in his chest.

"Oh, you know—working to corral corruption and put bad guys behind bars."

"Doin' your job then." He coughed. "You get your copy of *Cycle Mania* yet?"

"Nope. Hoping it comes in today. Anything good?" Harper tapped her user ID and password into the network portal, absently listening to her dad ramble about the latest innovations for the big choppers they used to work on together. An unexpected sensory memory swamped her and she could smell the rich exhaust of an old Kawasaki H1 500 engine, could feel the smooth glide of cloth over chrome.

She'd loved motorcycles since she was a kid, always interested in the hows and the whys. It had given her a connection with her dad, a way to gain his attention and earn his approval. When had he first let her near the machines he'd made his living from? Absently interrupting him, she asked. "How old was I when I started helping you out at the shop, Dad?"

He snorted. "Couldn't a been more than four. Showed up with one a them Cracker Jack temporary tattoos on your arm, proud as hell and showing it off to all the guys. Without even asking, you grabbed a cloth and set yourself to polishing the tailpipes of that '72 FLH Shovelhead Hardtail I was chopping. Like you were part of the crew. Had a soft spot for that bike ever since." He paused, his breathing slightly labored from years of smoking. "It's been a long time since I laid hands on anything that makes my heart speed up like that bike."

"Good thing Mom's not around to hear you say that," she teased, clicking to open the desktop file labeled Beaux Hommes. She scribbled a couple of notes on a legal pad and switched the screen to her email inbox.

"She's working overtime at the store this week," he grumbled.

Harper knew just how much it bothered him that his wife had been forced to work at their local grocery store after the custom cycle shop her dad and his two brothers had built went under. Her old man had worked for as long as Harper could remember to design the next big thing in the motorcycle industry, always sure he was on cusp of some great financial payout. It had never come through. He'd been forced to start letting staff go just before Harper left for college, one man at a time. Two years after she'd graduated, he and his brothers closed the doors for good.

It had been just as much of a blow to Harper as it had been for her dad. She'd lived that dream with him, worked side by side to learn the trade, designing custom bikes, running the wrench or the paint gun, managing the books and, like him, always waiting for that one chance to make it big.

Which was why when her former lover, Marcus, offered to help her recognize the family dream, she'd jumped on board. And been screwed over.

Her email pinged. The sound jolted her from rapidly spiraling memories, and the phone slipped from her grasp. Fumbling, she caught it before it hit the desk and put the receiver to her ear. "Sorry. Got a little nostalgic for a second, Dad."

"Nostalgic, my ass. You were thinking about Marcus. You ever hear he gets paroled, let me know. I may be old, but no one's got to puree my peas yet, and my trigger finger's still in fine shape." The man's hostility rolled over the line and through her consciousness, the familiar threat both soothing and terrifying.

"We've been over this, Dad. I'm a federal officer now, so no threatening to off anyone when we talk, yeah?"

"Some days I wish you'd joined the mafia instead of the IRS."

"Funny guy." She absently scanned the email that had just landed in her inbox and froze. It was what she'd been waiting for—the green light to move on the strip club. And she'd been named the lead investigator. Three months of subtle but hard work and endless hours of research had finally paid off. She was going to take these guys down.

She interrupted her old man. "I've got to go, Dad. Work's calling. I'll be out of town for a few days, but I'll call soon."

"Be careful, baby girl," he said, voice husky.

"Always. Love you both." She hung up, already out of her chair and in motion. Gathering the loose files on her desk, she shoved them and her laptop into her beat-up messenger bag. Daniel nearly ran her over as he charged into her cubicle as she headed out.

He grinned. "You get the email?"

"Yep," she said with an answering smile. "I'm cleared for Seattle."

"They're giving you the lead on this one. It's about time. You earned it."

"Thanks." She swallowed hard. "You're still on the case, though."

"Yeah. I'll follow you in a week—sooner if you need me—and we'll wrap up whatever you've got, get the local field office involved for cleanup and close the case. Standard fare, but this is your first time flying solo, Harper." He studied her with a decidedly calculated look. "You cool?"

"Cool? Man, she's colder than the Arctic in January," a voice muttered over a near cubicle wall.

"You know, just because you *have* a dick doesn't give you carte blanche to *act* like one," she snapped. Still, the guy's barb stung.

As the only female investigator in this division, she'd expected to have to smash some glass ceilings, but she hadn't anticipated the outright animosity she'd faced from her peers and, in some cases, superiors.

Yes, she'd once been investigated herself by the IRS's criminal investigative unit, but she'd been exonerated completely.

And seeing that process in action, observing the security with which the agents had done their jobs, had prompted her to pursue the kind of financial stability she'd never known growing up. Dreams were great, but they didn't pay the mortgage or put food on the table. So she'd put her accounting degree to work for the very entity that had proven to her that policy and procedure could give her a different type of satisfaction.

Daniel, the only coworker who'd shown her any level of genuine camaraderie over the years, offered her a hand and tipped his chin in the direction the slight had come from. "I'll deal with that later."

"Don't bother." One corner of her mouth kicked up. "On a scale of one to infinity, my witty factor will always be higher than most of these guys' sperm counts."

He laughed, ignoring the sputtering of a couple of voices nearby. "You really should have ditched the rules and gone out with me when I asked."

"Yeah, well, I'm still of the opinion that if you break the rules, you own the consequences. Besides, I wasn't ready for that kind of commitment." And after Marcus, she probably never would be.

He considered her, his eyes searching her face. "What would it take to make you break the rules?"

"Nothing short of a life-changing experience—and I'm not looking for that kind of commitment, either." Daniel reached for her but she stepped out of range. "I'll catch the red-eye to Seattle first thing in the morning and check in after I get a feel for the place. Keep a bag packed on the off chance I have to call you in early."

"I'll pack as soon as I get home." He tipped his head toward the lobby and spoke so low Harper had to lean in to hear him. "Don't go out there with the idea you've got something to prove to these desk jockeys, Harper. That's how people end up getting in over their heads."

"I'm almost six feet tall *without* heels, so the odds of me getting in over my head are slim to none. Tell the director I'm out and I'll be in touch after I wrap the first day."

She started for the lobby, her stride long and sure. The anomalous snap of her stiletto heels on the thin industrial carpet was muted but still set her apart from the muffled shuffle of men's dress shoes. She couldn't care less. She'd been given her first solo assignment, and she was going to work—and close—this case with her notorious efficiency.

For a brief second, she felt sorry for the strippers at Beaux Hommes. She hated to see people lose their jobs. But corruption couldn't be stopped otherwise. They could dance at other clubs.

The owners, on the other hand, the men she suspected were using the club as a front to move large amounts of cash? Harper intended to make those men pay the highest possible price for their lies and corruption.

And to her, the price to be paid for deception was never high enough.

LEVI WALSH PROPPED his elbows on the small desk and tunneled his fingers through his hair. A monstrous headache had settled on his temples. If it kept evolving at this rate, it would become a full-blown migraine before the club opened its doors later tonight. Considering he was the marquee dancer this evening, he couldn't afford the complication. Because Levi was in deep shit.

He'd bought into the club as a 25-percent owner six weeks ago. After the three other owners discovered Levi was an investment whiz, they'd encouraged him to check out the books. They didn't realize he'd been the kid who'd gone to the University of Washington at age sixteen and then the Foster School of Business for his postgraduate degree at age twenty. They only knew him as the shy boy who'd been thrust onto the stage during open-call night on a fraternity dare. The other dancers had bet against him surviving the experience. He'd taken their money right down to the last dime. He'd enjoyed working at the club and believed in its earnings potential. Even so, prior to the purchase, Levi had taken a couple of days and done an in-depth review of the profit-and-loss statements and both the digital and manual-entry ledgers. The club turned out to be a bigger moneymaker than he'd estimated, so he'd bought in. It had nearly wiped out his and his parents' investment funds, but the returns should have been immediate.

But then, just days after he'd signed the contracts, he'd learned via a passing comment from the general manager about a third ledger, one the guy used to track "daily stuff" before entering firm numbers into the formal ledgers. That had made Levi very uneasy. Since then, he'd had been bugging the general manager, Kevin Metcalf, to hand over that third ledger.

It had taken almost a month to corner him, but Levi had caught Kevin in the main office this morning and demanded the ledger, no excuses. Kevin had handed it over and retreated to his private office without a word.

Now that the manual-entry book was in his hands, though, Levi was sorry he'd pressed. Something was seriously wrong. Granted, he was busted-ass tired after having been up all night entertaining Sarah—or was it Tara? Whatever. He wasn't nearly so tired he couldn't decipher simple double-entry bookkeeping ledgers.

Leaning forward again, he parked his head in his hands and tried to view the ledger entries from a different perspective. It didn't help. They didn't add up. "What a freakin' mess."

The club's general manager ought to be whipped with the electrical cord from an adding machine for the mess he'd made of this thing. There should be checks and crosschecks to ensure nothing was omitted, skipped or forgotten. Not in this case. How the company managed to function blew his mind. That he depended on it for roughly half of his monthly income? His gut cramped.

The digital files he'd reviewed had led him to believe the club was raking in the cash. If he'd seen this third ledger, he would have abandoned the deal before he reached the end of the book's first page. Levi had made a very bad and very costly mistake.

Picking up his cell, he hit speed dial for the direct number to Jeff Wheaton, the owner Levi was most familiar with. The alcohol distributor was also the owner who'd originally approached Levi about buying in.

The man answered on the second ring. "Wheaton."

"Jeff, it's Levi."

"What's up, man?"

"Have you seen the manual ledger—the *third* ledger—Kevin keeps for the club?" The pause on the other end stretched out so long Levi checked his phone's screen to ensure the call hadn't dropped. "Did I lose you, Jeff?"

The guy cleared his throat. "Apologies. I was trying to remember whether I'd ever seen his working ledger."

Levi blew out a hard breath. "This isn't a *working ledger*, Jeff. This is a mess of epic proportions. There's no way the P&L sheets and the digital ledger can be right if Kevin's entering figures from this thing."

"I'm sure it's fine, Levi."

"And I'm sure it's proof the books aren't right," he bit out.

"How can you be sure?" It sounded as though Jeff was speaking through a clenched jaw.

"I'm looking at his ledger right now. The guy has alcohol purchases categorized as income, payroll written in and then written over multiple times in ink so there's no telling what the right numbers are, and quarterly tax payments have been deducted more than once. I'm on page *one*." Levi closed his eyes and scrubbed a hand over his forehead. "It's royally screwed up."

"If it will give you peace of mind, I'll make a couple of calls, get in touch with Mike and Neil, and find out what the accountants have been apprised of," Jeff said, his words strung tight and close together. "In the meantime, why don't you get together with Kevin and ask him about his methods?"

The headache tightened its invisible metal band, crushing Levi's skull. "Just keep me posted."

"Of course."

The distinct click of the call disconnecting sounded louder than it likely was. Levi swiped a thumb across the screen to make sure his phone was off before tossing it onto the paper-littered desk. Slowly rising, he kept his hands braced on the desk and let his head hang loose as he took a few slow breaths.

There's an easy answer to this mess. The club's never missed payroll, never had vendor issues. No way is it as bad as it seems. Just my paranoia. I would've noticed if something had been wrong, really wrong, when I reviewed the books.

He hoped.

Lifting his face, Levi slid his glasses down and, rubbing the bridge of his nose, shouted as loud as he could manage without cracking his head wide-open. "Hey, Kevin!"

Nothing but silence.

He'd find the guy and drag him in here, get him to explain the convoluted system Levi hoped and prayed was being used. "Kevin!"

Still no answer.

Shoving his glasses on, he stalked out of the tiny closet–cum–side office and glanced around.

Empty.

What the hell? Where did everyone go? And when?

A sharp knock startled him. He strode to the door and opened it a few inches, bracing his foot and shoulder on the back side to prevent being rushed. "Yeah?"

"Open the door, please."

The woman's voice was as smooth as fine whiskey and hot as smoke-fueled sin. Levi drew in a sharp breath. Then her foot hooked around the edge of the door to expose a length of leg that could have tempted an angel to fall. And he was no angel. He wanted to trace his fingers from the arch exposed in the cutaway heels all the way to her—

"I'll ask once more. Open the door, please."

Levi cleared his throat. "Club opens at nine tonight. Come back then."

She laughed, the sound rich and throaty. "Right. Open the door. Now."

The authority that infused her voice made Levi's brows draw down, pulling the skin over his temples and making his headache even more pronounced. "Shit."

"That's closer to the response I expected. You know who I am?"

"No clue. I've got a headache."

"Isn't that usually my gender's line?" she asked drolly.

"Cute. Seriously, club's not open." He moved his foot just as she shoved. The door nailed him in the forehead, the impact splitting his skull. Stumbling away from the door, he bent forward at the waist and clutched his head. "Son of a bitch."

"Now that? That's more the greeting I'm used to."

He slowly stood, his gaze traveling over the longest legs he'd ever seen, over the trim swell of hip and the tight nip of waist, over a pair of what had to be heaven-sanctioned breasts and up to stunning gray eyes. Ringed in sooty lashes, those eyes were cool, almost cold, and hidden behind benign, '50s-style men's glasses. She hadn't played up the pixie cap of black hair that framed a face almost devoid of makeup. Her full lips curled down at the corners.

"You got your fill yet?"

"Huh?"

"C'mon. I realize the door caught you on the head, but it wasn't nearly hard enough to warrant me breaking out the hand puppets." She blinked slow, smiled slower. "Unless, of course, your head is as thick as it seems, based on the sound it made on impact."

"Thick?"

"Head, door, thickheaded."

Levi chuffed out a short breath. "You think I'm stupid?" The idea entertained him. It also made him want to prove her wrong. The longer he thought about it, the more her assertion pissed him off. "Rather juvenile assumption. You've spent less than three minutes in my presence."

She waved the comment off and glanced around the office. "I need to speak to a manager."

"I qualify." He didn't elaborate.

"Are you the manager?"

"I'm the only employee here, so it's me or no one."

"Looks like today's just not your day, handsome."

"Why?" he asked absently, massaging the knot forming on his forehead.

One corner of her mouth curled up. "I really have to speak to someone with authority."

"And I told you I'm your only option at the moment." Shrugging off the pain, he pulled his glasses off and arched one brow disdainfully. "You've become the bane of my existence in record time. Now, who are you, princess?"

She grinned, the expression so feral Levi fought not

to take a step back. "Princess? Not terribly original, are you." A quick flip of the wrist and she'd unclipped a bifold ID holder at her waist and held it out for him to read. He slipped his glasses on again and immediately wished he hadn't.

"My name is Harper Banks. I'm a senior criminal investigator with the Internal Revenue Service." She handed him a sealed envelope. "Beaux Hommes is under investigation for suspected tax evasion and fraud."

Shit.

2

HALF OF HARPER'S brain was mentally peeling this guy's clothes off because, *damn*, he was gorgeous. The other half demanded she forgo the mental stripper scene and simply dress him down. No way was an attractive face going to derail her field investigation before it really began.

She clipped her government ID on her hip and glanced around the office. The place was nice if you ignored the layer of dust on the fake plants and the general disorganization of what she presumed was the receptionist's desk. Generic office furniture appeared relatively new, the visible technology more so. MacBooks and color laser printers sat idle on several desktops while somewhere deeper in the office suite, a telephone rang. But the file cabinets were out of sight, and that's where she wanted to start.

The weight of the man's stare was both hot and cold, curious and furious when she shifted toward him. The way he considered her, so intense and controlled, dragged an involuntary shiver up her spine.

"Uncomfortable?"

"It's eighty-three degrees outside. I'm wearing a long-sleeved shirt because your weatherman forecasted early winter temperatures last night."

"So, not physically cold." He crossed his arms. "What's the problem, then?"

Harper considered him, wondering how he could still be so inexplicably sexy in a simple pair of glasses and baggy sweats. And when he lost the glasses and donned the attitude? Things south of the belt went on alert. "I'm not the one with the problem…"

"Levi."

"Levi what?"

"Levi Walsh."

Her eyes snapped to his face before she could stop the reaction. *Interesting.* So she'd nabbed the newest owner right out of the box. Lucky her.

She considered how to play this. She could tell him straight out that she knew he was the club's newest co-owner. But he'd likely shut down and wait for the troops before talking to her. Not productive.

The other option was to go along with his game, pretend ignorance and see how much he volunteered. He might play nice if he didn't feel cornered. Yet not owning up to the fact that she recognized him was a lie of omission, and she didn't know if she could accept that kind of near deceit.

He watched her, widening his stance. Not quite combative but not friendly, either. "So what's the protocol?"

"What are you, ex-military? 'Protocol,'" she said on a snort, mind racing to another option than the lie.

He whipped off his glasses, pale blue eyes alight with irritation. "You can be as much of a smart-ass as you'd like, Ms. Banks, but don't lord your authority over me like I'm some two-bit chump here to take your beating."

"Quite the speech." She tugged at her sleeves, ensuring her wrists were covered. "Beaux Hommes is being investigated—"

"Based on what? Anonymous tip? Filing discrepancies? What was the red flag that sent you haring across the country to make my life hell?"

Drawing a deep breath, she forced the clenched muscles in her jaw to relax. "If you'll let me finish?"

He dipped his chin once.

"Gracious of you. Thanks." Even in her heels, this guy topped her by an easy two inches, making her have to stand up straighter and lift her chin in order to meet his gaze. "Everything is outlined in the letter I handed you, but I'll summarize."

"Gracious of you," he parroted, his sarcasm as thick as cold syrup and just as distasteful.

"The IRS lives to serve." Hands resting below her belly button, she gripped her opposite wrist. "Beaux Hommes had a variety of red flags—a radical drop in revenue, excessive expenses in relation to that annual revenue, a significant increase in employees disparate to the drop in revenue and tip reporting discrepancies on official documents."

She paused, gauging his reaction. The guy actually appeared surprised by her list, but she'd seen too much over the past few years to buy a ticket to that particular show. Still, the expression on his face wasn't the deer-in-the-headlights, oh-man-I'm-*so*-busted look most audit recipients sported. He seemed concerned but curious, and that curiosity threw her for a loop. She hated loops.

"Seems like an awful lot of suspicion for a single year's return."

Smart, she mused. Or it had been a lucky guess. "As I said, the letter explains everything."

His eyes roved over her and she had the distinct impression he was using the borderline rude action to buy time to formulate his response. Too bad she didn't feel like accommodating him.

Releasing her hands so they hung by her side, she

blinked slowly. "This conversation has been great, but I have to speak to the manager on duty. Now."

"I manage the dancers, and I'm the only one here. You'll have to make do with me."

His lie decided her course of action. He'd implied he was nothing more than a midlevel manager. She needed access to the files as soon as possible if she was going to close this case, so they'd play it his way. "Your day just gets worse and worse, doesn't it? First, I'd like to see the operating ledgers, as well as P&L statements for the last three years. Digital or paper copies will be fine. Current and past employee files would be helpful, too."

"I don't actually work in this department."

And there it is. The first blatant, outright lie. She'd learned that the guilty regularly manipulated the truth into something they thought would offer them the most hope of escape. Knowing this firsthand didn't squelch the sting of disappointment that he'd followed the pattern, though. She had…what? Hoped he might be honorable?

"Get over yourself," she muttered softly enough he didn't hear her.

He looked over his shoulder at the large wall clock. "I'm guessing everyone has gone to lunch. If you want to come back in an hour or so, I can get you in touch with the general manager, Kevin Metcalf. He'll be able to help you with whatever you need."

"I'm not leaving until I see those files. I have my own computer, but I'll need access to a dedicated printer and copier." He looked at her blankly, and she sighed. "Do you have *any* idea where the P&Ls or ledgers might be?"

He sighed. "I'll have to make a couple of calls."

"Feel free, but I'm within my jurisdiction to begin my investigation even without your help. It'll save both of us a lot of time if you'd point me in the right direction."

He shifted to sit on the desk behind him, crossing his arms over his chest. "Should I obtain legal representation?"

Harper strolled to the desk opposite Levi and leaned a hip against it, considering him. "You're free to do so, but retaining an attorney won't stop me from looking over company files and copying relevant paperwork. Even a court-ordered injunction won't be enough. The IRS has authority in this investigation, Mr. Walsh."

His eyes flashed even as his lips thinned. "You're making it very hard for me to want to comply."

She lifted one shoulder in an approximation of a shrug meant to irritate. "Not my problem." For some reason, needling him was entertaining. "My job is to uphold the law and execute the actions detailed in that letter."

"Nice." He ripped the envelope open, scanned the letter and made a very visible effort to keep himself from reacting. When he looked up, he'd mastered his emotions again. "I'm going to make those calls before I give you the proverbial keys to the kingdom. You can wait here or outside." He shoved off the desk and stalked to a tiny room off the reception area, not waiting for her response before slamming the door behind him.

"I'll be right here," she murmured. He had an air about him, a subtle confidence she found inexplicably attractive.

Reminding herself what was at stake, she began mentally cataloging the office. Digging into her briefcase, she pulled out her iPad and began tapping in visible inventory and taking supporting pictures. Seven desks with one computer each, yet none of the desks had any paperwork on them, save for the very first desk, where the sole phone rested. There were four printers, only one of which was actually plugged in. The others had a faint covering of dust and a general air of disuse. *Interesting.*

Logging it all, she wandered through the desks, randomly opening drawers and searching for any signs of use. Again, only the first desk seemed occupied.

"Who sits here?" she called out.

Levi emerged from the small office, smartphone pinned between his ear and shoulder as he flipped through the letter. "Sure. That makes sense." He paused, glancing at her as he spoke. "No, she's not the most agreeable person I've ever met." He laughed. "You'd think, but it appears she's unaffected by my many charms." Another laugh. "Yeah, well, some women are completely immune to men."

Harper blinked slowly. "Are you implying I'm a lesbian simply because I'm not falling at your feet and begging you to take me?"

He stopped, his gaze heating as it roamed over her body. As he pulled the cell phone from his shoulder, one corner of his mouth kicked up in a roguish smile. "Nope, but I *would* say you let your professional ambitions ruin any fun you might have. Probably ever."

Marcus had accused her of being too ambitious, too anxious to push the next project. He'd claimed she'd been domineering and that had driven him to seek *true* feminine solace with their company's receptionist. That's when she'd realized how stupid she'd been—made even more painfully obvious when she, Marcus and their other partner, Vigo, were arrested for embezzlement and fraud.

But she wasn't that gullible kid anymore. Her successes were *hers*. A woman in a man's world, she wasn't about to apologize for her professional drive or explain to Levi that she had plenty of fun. She'd prove it to him.

She let one corner of her mouth curl up. "Tell me, Levi. If you don't work in this particular department, where *do* you work?"

"I'm employed by the club." His eyes tightened at the admission, revealing the very early markers of crow's-feet. "Why?"

She crossed her arms under her breasts, and his gaze dropped to the glimpse of cleavage the button-up shirt exposed. "I'm wondering how Beaux Hommes most benefits from your particular brand of charm, unpolished as it is." She blinked slowly. "I'd assume whatever you do doesn't require much talking."

Shifting his attention to somewhere over her shoulder, he snorted. "Forget it, Ms. Banks. I'm not stupid enough to bait this particular dragon. I'm just trying to supplement my income."

"So is Beaux Hommes your regular source of income?"

He eyed her with open distrust. "Sort of."

"Do you dance to earn that income?" she asked, coquettishly tipping her head to one side. "That would require mastery of seduction."

Levi scowled at her and tugged his collar. "I'm actually…"

Harper held her breath. She'd opened the door for him, giving him an easy way to offer her the truth.

He dropped his hands to his waist and looked at the floor. "I *am* a dancer. The lead dancer, actually. I got into it to support my parents after…after they…" He stumbled to a conversational halt. "What I earn here helps them out."

She shifted from foot to foot. Something about his answer, the way he tripped over it, bothered her. "What happened with your parents, Levi?"

Lifting his chin, he considered her before laughing again, decidedly softer this time. "I'm not interested in whatever angle you're trying to work." His face tightened. "As for my parents? Don't go there. They're off the table and off-limits. Period."

"I'm an IRS agent. I don't *work angles*," she bit out, "and I go where I have to go." His response only made her more curious, more concerned. But pitying this man or his parents wasn't going to close the case.

Irritation rode her spine like a free-fall carnival ride,

climbing one vertebra at a time only to career down her back and haul her stomach with it. She was caught between wanting to prove him wrong and…what? Wanting to force him to understand that she was human, too?

Harper stilled. *Where had* that *come from?* She didn't know him, wouldn't ever see him again after this case closed, yet it mattered what he thought of her in that particular moment? "No," she said softly, shaking her head, unaware she'd spoken aloud until he responded.

"No, what?"

"It doesn't matter," she muttered, totally thrown off balance for the first time since taking this job.

Levi considered her, the look on his face both shrewd and calculating. "Suddenly not up to the verbal sparring? That means you forfeit this round, Ms. Banks. Can your ego take it?"

Her mouth opened and closed twice before she got her voice back. "You do *not* want to challenge me, Mr. Walsh. I'll take you to the mat."

"Yeah?" He pulled his glasses off and grinned. "What will you do with me then?"

Harper realized too late that he'd walked her right into the flirtatious byplay. Fighting the urge to snarl, she held out one hand and curled her fingers. "The ledger."

"I was hoping you'd be more creative than that."

Something suspiciously close to attraction curled around her ankles and made its way up her legs. "I'll ask one last time, Mr. Walsh. What is it *exactly* that you do for Beaux Hommes?"

His eyes grew hooded. Tossing his glasses onto the desk behind him, he slowly pulled his sweatshirt off to reveal a wickedly cut torso, his obliques so defined they were like funnels for the eyes, drawing them straight to…*whoa.*

Harper lost her battle to subdue a heated blush. "I get

the picture. If you're a stripper, though, why are you working in the office?"

His face closed down. "They keep the *Hooked on Phonics* set in the closet for us to come by and use whenever we want."

"I didn't mean it that way," she fumbled, beyond irritated that she'd so completely lost her footing. She'd known he was a stripper. She just hadn't expected him to own it with such authority—or to demonstrate it.

"Yeah? Well, you're a bright woman. Choose your words more carefully when you make snap judgments."

"Right. Because I'm sure you were in there with the ledger, what, fixing it? I didn't know LeapFrogs had Excel spreadsheet capabilities. My bad."

His shoulders went rigid. "Stop assuming I'm stupid."

"Then stop using your body as your primary asset!"

And that, right there, was the problem. She'd assumed he was harmless. She wouldn't make that mistake again.

LEVI'S MUSCLES LOCKED UP. From the bottom of his feet to the top of his scalp. She had pissed him off with that last allegation, that he used his body as his primary asset. Yes, he was a stripper, but he was more than that. He wasn't a brainless body. If that's what she thought, though? His lips thinned and his eyes narrowed.

She was also with the IRS. He had a personal history with that arm of the government, which made defying her way more satisfying.

"Enough with the evasive maneuvers. Give me the ledger, Mr. Walsh." She tugged.

His hands fisted, the letter crinkling in protest. "I'll get it for you." *At least the one I intend to show you.* "But for doing so, I'd appreciate little show of good faith." *Show...* "Why don't you come to the show tonight?"

"I don't… No," she stammered. "That's not my flavor of entertainment."

"How can you be sure? Have you ever been to a male revue?" He leaned back and waited.

"Hand over the ledger, Mr. Walsh. And please put your clothes on again. It's not appropriate for you to use your body as a deterrent to this investigation."

"Couple of big words in there for such a simple mind as mine." He stood and slowly untied the string of his sweatpants, working the material down to expose the skin of one hip. "I'd think something like this would qualify as more of a deterrent than a simple bare chest."

"Cut it out, Levi," she barked, twisting away from him. "I'm going to arrest you if you don't cut the crap right now."

"I'm not impeding anything. I've invited you to the show tonight. I'll get the ledger from…the owner I just spoke to and make copies for you. Besides, don't you want to see firsthand how the club operates?" Leaning on the desk, he left his sweats riding low and tightened his abs, sure she wouldn't be able to keep herself from looking.

She spun further away, immediately proving him right.

Tightening his glutes made his hips shift forward. "Ms. Banks?"

Her eyes went to his groin right before a faint blush stole across her cheeks. "Stop it."

"If you want to see how we handle cash income, you have to come to a show and document our practices." He straightened, tugging his pants up as he went. "I'm right, and you know it."

Harper shook her head. "What I *know* is that you're pressing me to come watch you take your clothes off. What I *don't* know is why. What do you hope to gain?"

A chance. The answer popped into Levi's head unbidden. Yes, he needed the chance to fix the ledgers. But there was also something about this woman that made him want her to have a little fun, even if it went against her better judgment. He and the guys specialized in good times.

Considering her, he kept his gaze cool and detached. "I don't expect to get anything out of it other than a fair chance to document the club's business practices." *And to try to figure out what Kevin did to the damn ledger to make it look like a scratch pad for a first-year English major taking graduate-level accounting—before Harper gets to it.*

A fine sheen of sweat popped out on Levi's upper lip and along his hairline. His stomach pitched and rolled like a dinghy in a violent storm. If she got her hands on the ledger, she could shutter the business. Which meant he was out of a job.

While he didn't count on stripping for his entire income, most of the money he made at the club went into his parents' investment portfolio. He'd supported them since his dad, a third-generation farmer, had lost everything after four consecutive drought years. Then the corn subsidies dried up. His dad hadn't been able to pay the taxes on the land, so the IRS had taken everything from him and auctioned it off to settle the debt. His dad, the man Levi had admired all his life, had been reduced to working at a fast-food restaurant while Levi's mom had taken a job at a big-box store as a greeter.

It enraged Levi. Here he was working his ass off to make sure his parents were taken care of, and the IRS showed up *again*. It struck him as far too personal. He'd watched his parents go through this once before, and he'd be damned if he'd watch it happen again.

That meant he had to keep one IRS investigator otherwise occupied until he fixed Kevin's daily accounts ledger. Levi was absolutely willing to flirt, even tease her a bit if it distracted Harper long enough. He wouldn't seduce her, though. Even as much as he despised the IRS, there were some things a man just didn't do, and using sex as a manipulative weapon was up there near the top of that list.

Of course, if the club was guilty of fraud, he could be facing asset seizure and jail time. Levi would lose everything. His parents would lose everything all over again. No cost was too high to stop that from happening.

"Mr. Walsh?" Harper asked, considering him. "You're sweating. Did you spring an unexpected fever or is your conscience suddenly manifesting?"

"My conscience is fine." He swallowed, feeling more off balance than he had since she'd nearly caved in his skull with the door. "It's hot in here."

"Considering you're not wearing your shirt and the air-conditioning is running, I'm putting my money on conscience." She tucked her hands in her skirt pockets. "What's got you so worried?"

"Nothing. I know the reporting practices are sound." The lie slipped out without a thought.

"If I come to the show tonight, you'll bring me that ledger?"

Without batting an eye, Levi held out a hand. "Agreed."

He watched the investigator from hell hesitate before reaching out and shaking his hand, her gaze both shrewd and wary. "That was a little too easy. If you've misled me in any way, I *will* discover it, Mr. Walsh. And when I do, I'll prosecute you to the fullest extent of the law for impeding a federal officer in the execution of her duties. Are we clear?"

His stomach plummeted even as he slowly locked stares with the one woman capable of making him hate his life. "Do your worst."

"Oh, I will," she answered softly, picking up her briefcase and heading for the front door. "I will."

Levi had absolutely no doubt that she, at least, wasn't hedging the truth.

3

HARPER COULD ONLY imagine the razzing she was going to get from the men in the office when they found out she'd gone to a show at Beaux Hommes. After all, she'd been pretty insistent she'd rather audit God than deal with muscle-bound men clad in G-strings and slathered in testosterone. Galling as it was, though, Levi had been right. The best way to see the club's practices in action was to get inside during operating hours. So here she stood, assessing her wardrobe for clubbing attire.

She couldn't help but roll her eyes at irony's sense of humor.

Not having brought anything really appropriate for a night out, she was stuck piecing together what she could from her suitcase. One pair of low-slung skinny jeans, one pair of black platform heels and a white dress shirt with French cuffs proved the best she could do on short notice.

She fully expected Levi to put his sensual talents to good use. The image of him pulling his shirt off and easing his pants down was seared in her brain, damn him.

But for every action, there was an equal and opposite reaction. Assuming Levi intended to attempt to seduce her, her reaction was hers to control. She could play a little suggestive cat and mouse with him. She'd never take it far enough to be accused of improper behavior. He wasn't worth losing her job over. But she was willing to take things to the very edge of the gray zone in order to retain the upper hand and control the outcome—a successful closure of this case.

For a brief moment, she wondered what her dad would think of her willingness to manipulate someone to achieve her goal. He'd be disappointed she hadn't chosen to be a better person than the opposition. But then, that was why he was poring over pictures of bikes in magazines instead of working on them himself.

She grabbed her keys and left her hotel room. It had been ages since she'd tried to flirt with someone. Her mouth was dry enough to be declared a federal disaster area. And one eye twitched. She pressed her fingers near the edge of her eye, trying not to mess up her makeup.

Tonight was going to be all about sex without touching, innuendo without crossing invisible lines and suggestions without follow-through. She'd be on Levi's turf, so she'd have to up her game, insecurities and history be damned.

The drive passed in a blur of GPS directives, and shaking off the last of her self doubt, she pulled up to the club. The line of women waiting to get inside surprised her. Cover was twenty bucks a head. Freaking crazy. Yet within ten minutes she was in the mass of estrogen waiting her turn to get her wrist stamped and pass through security.

Once inside, she was reluctantly impressed. The club was clean, well lit and tastefully decorated. It wasn't as if she'd expected giant statues of Priapus to grace every square inch of free floor space, but she also hadn't expected the fine art pieces, the comfortable seating areas or the subtle sense of wealth the interior projected. Not even close. There wasn't anything seedy about the place. It made some of the reports she'd received more curious than ever. How could Beaux Hommes be involved in illegal business practices and still project such a sense of accomplishment? It broke every stereotypical assumption she'd had.

"Can I get you something to drink?"

Forcing herself to turn slowly, she wasn't entirely surprised to find a waiter clad in tuxedo pants, a bow tie and shirt cuffs. She *was* surprised to find him maintaining eye contact despite the cleavage she was sporting.

He winked at her with an air of innocent flirtation. "Maybe a margarita? Or are you more a white-wine kind of lady?"

"I'm actually more a shot of Patrón with a beer chaser kind of woman." The honesty of her answer surprised her. Not that she would have lied, but had she thought about it, she would have simply ordered a sparkling water and been done with it.

"Shot of Patrón it is. What kind of beer, beautiful?"

She smiled slowly, watching the man's eyes soften as he stared at her mouth. "How about a Michelob Ultra in the bottle."

"First drink's on me," he murmured. "My name's Donovan. You need anything tonight, you find me or shout out. I'm your man."

Uh-huh. Me and anyone else with a decent figure and a generous tipping habit. "Sure. I'll buy my drinks, though I appreciate the offer."

"You want a table?"

"Table?"

"Near the stage." He tucked his serving tray under his arm as he angled his head toward the front of the club. "Those are the best seats in the house. We always keep a few available for favored patrons."

She met his gaze, steady and confident he was doing her a favor. "I've never been here before."

"All the more reason to sit near the stage. C'mon." He reached for her hand.

Stepping away, she took a deep breath. "I'd prefer to just hang out here and see what's what first." She reached out and rubbed his arm, trying to soften her rejection. "I can always find you if I want a seat at the front, right?"

"The offer stands, particularly for you." He gave a little bow. "Shot of Patrón and Michelob Ultra in the bottle on the way."

"Thanks." She shifted her attention to the buzz around the club, taking in the women's excitement, the swift business the bar was doing and the orderliness with which everything ran. The first was understandable. The latter two were surprises. Given what she'd seen of the offices earlier, she hadn't expected any sense of organization during the more chaotic regular business hours. She wasn't entirely sure what to make of it. Unexpected aspects of any investigation were always worth a second look, though.

Donovan returned with her drink order. She downed the Patrón, relishing the burn even as she placed the shot glass on the serving tray. The Michelob she sipped before digging a twenty out of her pocket and dropping it on the tray. "Keep the change."

He grinned, placing a hand over his heart. "She looks like a goddess, drinks Patrón and tips like she's waited tables before. You might just be the perfect woman."

"No woman's perfect." She patted his cheek. "Sweet sentiment, though."

"Shout if you want anything at all. I'll check in on you in a bit." Pocketing the twenty, he headed to the next table of women.

It bothered her on a very fundamental level that she hadn't been able to just take his compliment without feeling the need to dissuade him from the belief she was perfect. And that he'd mentioned her looks first really irritated her. She'd have to get over the hang-up if she hoped to win when she sparred with Levi tonight. And she always played to win.

The lights dimmed. She leaned against the wall, a small smile tugging at the corners of her mouth as the women in the club went wild.

TOWEL WRAPPED AROUND his hips, Levi stepped into the locker room. The guys were giving each other shit in typical fashion. He loved this part of the night, when his nerves were strung tight enough to make the muffled buzz from the crowd skate across his skin with a slightly abrasive touch. It thrilled him and, if he was honest, kept him nervous—scared?—enough to ensure he forced himself to seize his alter ego by the balls, get onstage and dance his ass off. Otherwise? The urge to just settle into the background and play with his day trades was almost overwhelming.

"Levi!" Several of the men shouted greetings. Only two walked up to him and shoulder bumped him, though.

Eric and Justin, his two best friends, were winding up their dancing careers after finding success in the nine-to-five world. Part of him was jealous, but it had nothing to do with their financial accomplishments. The envy that ate at him and made him feel like a total ass was based on the relationships the two men had found.

Eric and Cass had been together long enough that Eric was starting to talk about rings and lifetimes and houses.

Justin and Grace were already engaged, having loved each other far longer than the few months they'd been together.

Every time they all went out, Levi was the fifth wheel. That he was envying his boys was one thing That he was letting himself slip into feel-sorry-for-himself territory was another. Disgusted, he drove a fist into the locker.

Eric opened his adjoining locker. He didn't turn around when he asked, "Feeling a little violent tonight, Einstein?"

Levi snorted. "Seriously? You guys need to let the nickname go. I'm not the one with the doctorate." He completely ignored the questionable violence call. It was too close to the truth.

Justin popped Eric with his towel, dropping trou without blinking an eye. "I might have the doctorate, but you're the one with your own company set to make millions."

Eric nodded toward Levi. "And the captain of finance here is going to out-earn all of us with his giant brain and play trades."

Or dump them all into financial ruin. Levi gently banged his head against the locker, forgetting about his bruised forehead until the first shock of pain registered. "Ow."

"Man, what happened to your head?" Eric leaned in close. "You look like you met the wrong end of a two-by-four."

"Actually, it was the office door."

Eric winced. "What'd you do, trip over your IQ and run headlong into your potential?"

"No, you gossipy wench. I didn't. I happened to move at the same time—" he paused, looking around before mumbling "—at the same time the investigator from the IRS shoved her way in."

Eric and Justin both stilled.

Levi leaned against the locker and crossed his arms. "What's worse, Kevin kept the real ledger from me before I bought into the club." He glanced around, feeling ridiculously paranoid. The other men moved in closer. "I was going over it today when the agent from hell showed up."

"And?" Justin quietly pressed.

"Something's not right."

"Not right as in 'Kevin can't do basic math' or not right

as in 'We need to pack our stuff and get out before we're dragged down'?" Eric asked.

"I don't think we need to get out. Not yet, anyway. And you guys in particular should be fine. I'm part owner, though, which could get a little dicier. I spent the morning with the ledger and trust me when I tell you there's a good chance we're going to get tagged, and hard, for something more than a little tax hiccup."

Justin's brow creased. "Why?"

"The IRS sends auditors when they want to look into the books. This woman identified herself as an investigator and asked not only for the standard books but also for the personnel and financial files."

"Shit," both men said in unison.

"Not a word to anyone else."

"No way," Justin muttered.

Eric nodded once. "What he said."

Levi cocked his head to the side, listening to the music. "Your set just cued, Nick," he shouted to one of the other dancers.

"On my way, boss man."

"I'm after Nick, so I should get out there." Levi opened his locker and pulled out a military uniform. "How obvious is the bruise on my forehead?"

Justin dug around in his locker and pulled out a pen and scrap of paper. "I'll pass a quick note to the lighting guys and let them know not to run a purple or blue light over your set. Should be fine."

Thinking about his upcoming performance, he absently touched the bruise again. "Hey. Let me borrow a piece of paper and your pen when you're done."

"Sure." Justin scribbled out his note, retrieved another piece of paper and handed it and the pen over.

Levi quickly jotted down his own note and folded it twice, wrote a name on the outside and returned the pen.

"Thanks." Dropping his towel, he absently stepped into first his black G-string and then his rip-away fatigues. He sat on the bench and pulled on his combat boots and white undershirt. As the marquee dancer, he was onstage longer than most. He had a sexually suggestive song to entertain to, and he'd changed up the routine a little tonight to showcase his physicality. If Harper Banks proved brave enough to show up, he'd give her a show she'd never forget.

The crowd screamed as Nick took the stage.

"Keep this to yourselves, okay? Catch you guys later."

Traversing the dark hallways, he stepped over cords and cables, the butterflies in his stomach building. He was going to up the heat to cook the crow he intended to serve Harper Banks. She wanted to make snap judgments on his intellect based on his appearance, wanted to believe that his IQ was equivalent to his biceps circumference? Fine. Let her. Until then, she was going to want him. He'd make sure of it. Then he was going to clean up the books and go over them line by line with her, defending every debit and credit with calm aplomb. She could suck it.

A stagehand met him in the wings. He pressed the note into the guy's hand. "Find Donovan and give this to him as fast as you can. It's about my set."

The young man nodded, took the paper and disappeared down the side of the stage and into the crowd.

Rolling his head back and forth and then rotating his shoulders, Levi bounced on his toes and scanned the crowd as the emcee announced his routine.

"Ladies, you're in luck tonight. Who here has seen Levi work the stage?" Screams. "Sounds like you can't get enough of him. Well, the feeling's entirely mutual." The music started, an electronic beat with a woman's moans and gasps in the background. "Welcome Levi to the stage!"

The crowd went wild.

4

THE ENERGY FROM the crowd filtered through Harper, slowly bringing her away from the wall to stand at one of the few empty tables near the back. She was on her second beer— thank you, Donovan—and beginning to get into the show. The men were spectacular, the athleticism undeniable, the dance moves seriously hot. More than once she'd had to remind herself she was here to observe the club's business practices, not its men.

So far she hadn't spotted anything illegal happening on this side of the curtain, but the night was young. After the show, she'd make Levi take her backstage so she could see how the dancers were logging their cash tips because, from what she'd observed, the take was damned impressive.

The lights went down and the hum of the crowd built to a static white noise that made the fine hairs on her arms rise. Faint gunfire sounded over the speakers. A very patriotic musical introduction followed. Deep and rhythmic, the DJ's voice filled the room. "Welcome Levi to the stage!"

The crowd went wild.

"What is this, a freakin' rock concert?" she asked no one in particular. "If they start moshing, I'm out."

Looking over the crowd and through the mass of women

waving cash, she caught a glimpse of Levi. He wore a pair of military fatigues, a white undershirt, combat boots and a hat. Strapped to his arm was a knife large enough to fillet a moose. She was gaping at him and she didn't even care. This was *not* the geeky guy who'd fumbled through her arrival earlier. This was *not* the same man who'd taken his sweatshirt off in an attempt to distract her. There were flavors of him there, but no. This was *not* the same man.

The man onstage was a sexual machine. He moved with a type of confident awareness that he was *it*, and every woman in the place wanted him. There was a sexual… presence to him that made her rub her thighs together. A man like that would be talented in bed. He couldn't do that thing with his hips onstage if he hadn't done it with someone in bed.

"Probably a thousand times." Her words were lost among the sounds of the crowd. But they were a reminder that this was a bad idea. She never should have come to the club when she knew he'd be—

Her eyes bugged when he pulled the giant knife. Her gaze locked onto his torso as he sliced the knife up his shirt halfway and then slowly, slowly worked it into his arm sheath. All the while, he kept moving his lower body—hips thrusting, glutes flexing, thighs straining the tight material of his pants. Every movement gave the smallest glimpse of his abs and a seriously cut six-pack of muscle. Tanned skin revealed a sheen of sweat under the stage lights. He gripped the edges of the now cut shirt in each hand and did a little peep show.

Money rained around him.

Moving to the edge of the stage, he spread his feet and ripped his shirt off. A near brawl broke out when he threw it into the crowd.

"Who *is* this guy?" she muttered.

A hand touched her elbow and she almost came out of her skin.

Whirling, she found Donovan standing next to her with a third beer in one hand and a glow stick held above his head in the other. "You look like you could use this," he shouted over the noise.

She silently grabbed the cold beer and downed half of it, ignoring the almost nauseating way it sloshed in her empty stomach. There would be time for regret later. Right now? She had to get herself under control.

In no part of her planning had she considered she might actually *want* Levi. She was supposed to be controlling the situation and, thus, the case. What she was experiencing at the moment was far closer to taking a sharp corner at high speed—any control she wielded was marginal at best.

The crowd grew louder.

"I'm out," she shouted at Donovan, digging in her pocket for the bills to cover the drink.

He grinned. "You might have to stick around a few more minutes."

"Why?"

He jerked his chin at something over his shoulder. "You'll have to take it up with him."

She froze, her beer bottle halfway to her lips. "No."

"Oh, yeah, gorgeous. He's coming for you."

LEVI LEAPED OFF the stage and danced his way through the crowd to Harper. She had her back to him and wasn't moving. Tall and lean, her waist nipped in before flaring slightly over lush feminine hips. Her shoulders were a touch wide. The way her neck curved made him want to kiss her just there, at the shallow indent at the top of her spine.

Donovan leaned toward her and said something indiscernible.

She shook her head.

The waiter took her beer, looking both amused and uncertain as he moved away and lowered the glow stick. A swift lift of his chin urged her face the stage.

She didn't.

"Don't chicken out on me now, sweetheart," Levi shouted above the crazy noise level.

She turned, driven by the challenge.

Levi's breath hung in his chest. The words he'd been about to toss out fell flat at his feet. The woman he'd met today appeared absolutely *nothing* like the woman gazing up at him now through smoky eyes, with no glasses, full lips and sharp cheekbones—she was a complete and total knockout. Breasts that had been full earlier had been magically lifted so they were somehow more. Her shirt was tied at her waist to reveal taut abs. Tight-fitting jeans enhanced her long legs. And she wore the same heels that had knocked him out earlier. She was a pale-skinned beauty he'd totally underestimated.

One corner of her mouth curled up, and her brows slowly rose. "I'm not your sweetheart."

Gripping every ounce of pride he could muster, he reached out and traced one finger along her jawline. "You could be."

Her laughter was like the best cigar followed by a sip of expensive whiskey—rich, sultry, cultivated. Seductive. But her voice? It was the way a voice should sound after a good hour of foreplay. "I bet you say that to all the girls."

"That line's wasted on the girls. I save it for the women, and trust me, Ms. Banks, from where I stand? You're all woman." He closed the distance between them, wrapped his hand around her neck and leaned in. "You want backstage? You'll have to come with me."

"I don't have to have your help to get backstage."

"But I can make your life easier, and a whole lot more

fun." He kneaded his fingertips into the tense muscles that ran along her spine. *Not nearly as calm as she's putting on.* "C'mon."

He watched her closely, aware the moment the muscles in her neck went from tight to nearly rigid. Levi dropped his hand and stepped just out of reach. Holding out his hand, he curled his fingers in a come-here motion. She started to lift her hand in his direction then paused. She considered him for a moment before finally closing the distance. Their fingers touched, a simple brush of skin across skin. Awareness jolted through him, an electrical shock to his entire system. His breath came faster. His fingers twined around hers in a jerky movement. His focus narrowed.

Her eyes never left his.

Levi began to back toward the stage, pulling her along slowly. The noise level seemed to have decreased, reduced to little more than a buzz as he took precise steps, redirecting his path to the stage stairs. Nothing, and no one, existed in that moment but the woman he guided toward the stage. Everything else became secondary. His plan for a little cultivated teasing wasn't going to be enough anymore. This wasn't the woman he'd encountered earlier, the one he'd been so sure he could direct at will. No, the woman whose hand he now held had shown up in the equivalent of feminine armor tonight. She'd come prepared for a fight, and that was the last thing he'd expected. He needed to rethink his approach, figure out how to maintain control. That would take time—time he didn't have. His only choice was to move forward, to exercise extreme caution, to execute the subtle seduction and make her want him. The rest he'd improvise. It had to start somewhere, and given their location? His only choice was to dance for her.

Yanking her close, he thrilled when she planted her free

hand on his chest, her fingers reflexively curling into the pad of muscle there as she lifted her face to his.

He flexed his pec.

Her fingers spasmed and she huffed, her hot breath skating over his lips.

Drawing her closer, he spun her in a tight circle so she was the one to back up the steps, keeping her off balance and touching him. All that mattered was that she didn't stop.

The first step parked her breasts at eye level for him. Grinning, he kept her moving. She could either go where he directed her or tip over. Her choice.

"You're a real bastard," she muttered.

"Ya think?" Grinning up at her, he winked and stopped her in the middle of the stage. "Wait until I really get going."

Amusement flickered in her gaze before she snuffed it out.

"What's it going to take to get you to let your hair down a little, Ms. Banks?"

"You could stop calling me Ms. Banks, for one."

The sharp command was issued with an undertone of insecurity that surprised him. "Consider it done…Harper."

Her fingers flexed against his chest before she flattened them out and, palm over his heart, leaned in close. "Are you going to talk me to death, or are you going to get down to business?"

"Oh, this one isn't business, honey." He couldn't stop his smile widening as he moved around her with all the grace he could muster. "This one's just for fun."

She stood perfectly still, facing stage right.

Stopping behind her, he leaned in so his lips were a mere whisper from the shell of her ear. "What are your fantasies, Harper?"

A slight stiffening of her spine said she'd heard him over

the crowd's din. Without warning, she spun to face him and closed the distance between them, her chest pressed against his. "My fantasies aren't up for discussion."

He lowered his lips to within a hairbreadth of hers. "Then I'll have to go with my…highly…active…imagination." Every last word was punctuated by the sensual brush of his fingertips over her skin. He thrilled at the goose bumps that chased his touch.

The music changed to a distinctive techno beat. The suggestive lyrics heated his blood. Skating his hands down her arms, he shifted, took one hand and spun her out and away. Her eyes were wide, surprise evident in their gray depths. Clearly she hadn't expected him to go through with the dance. This would teach her to doubt him.

Levi dropped her hand and went to his knees, crawling toward her in time with the music's bass line. She shifted from foot to foot as he drew closer, her eyes darting left and then right. She scrubbed her hands on her thighs and swallowed. It almost looked as if she was fighting the urge to run. *Odd.* He'd taken her for a bit more adventurous than that.

He went to his belly at her feet and then rolled over. Grasping her ankles he spread her legs and slid between them, hips thrusting up, the short, sharp movements an unmistakable sexual pantomime. His vantage point gave him an uninterrupted view up the long, lean length of her body. He was tempted beyond measure to touch her.

So he did.

Running his hands up over her calves and down again nearly scrambled his brain cells. The bare skin across the tops of her feet appeared pale in the bright light. Hungry for skin-to-skin contact, he ran his fingertips from the tips of her shoes across the narrow expanse of bare skin and under the hem of her jeans to grip her ankles. He reveled in the silkiness of her skin for a moment before tracing his way down the sides of her shoes to her arches. The way she twitched thrilled him. No way could she say he wasn't getting to her. Likewise, he couldn't deny she was affecting him in a way no woman ever had.

Definite complication to a calculated seduction.

He'd deal.

Sliding through her legs, he went to his knees before scaling her body one handhold at a time. He was careful not to cross proprietary boundaries. That didn't mean he let her move away. No, with the firm grip of each hand he insisted she accept his touch. The tension radiating off her body said he was well on his way to accomplishing what he'd set out to do: cranking her up.

Groin brushing her ass, he danced for her, with her. He ran his hands around her waist and splayed them over the slim expanse of skin above her jeans and below the shirt hem she'd knotted above her waist.

Her belly fluttered beneath his touch, her breathing undeniably rapid.

Applying subtle pressure to her abs encouraged her to lean into him. Gentle direction to and fro got her moving her hips in time to the music. She had great rhythm, keeping up with his direction without difficulty. Bending forward, he wrapped his arms around her and caged her with his arms, his chest, his hips. "You've got moves."

She didn't answer.

He let her go with reluctance and moved around her. Reaching behind him, he took her hands and dragged them up his body to his neck and then, with deliberation, down his body to the top edge of his pants. He parked her fingers under the waistband and, with relish, undid the snap and teased the zipper down. The crowd screamed louder.

Her fingers caressed his abs.

His hips thrust forward of their own accord. *Damn it.* The goal was to wind her up, not the other way around.

He'd never had trouble remaining professional. Getting turned on by a dance was the equivalent of having no stamina in bed—the guys would give him hell if they figured out what was going on.

When her fingers slid lower and brushed the edge of his G-string, his whole body jerked and he lost the beat of the music for a moment.

Like that, is it?

No way would he allow her to take control of his show. No dice.

He took her wrists and encouraged her hands lower, then lower still. Her fingertips brushed the root of his swelling cock.

She jerked as if she'd been shoved.

Levi pulled her hands free and spun in the loose circle of her arms before indelicately shoving her hands down the back of his pants so her palms cupped the bare skin of his ass. With a couple of careful twists, he trapped her arms under his.

With her feet still spread, it was the work of a moment to position a thigh between her legs and press up, into her sex, as he took the dance to a whole new level. Her breasts brushed against his chest, capturing his attention. He dragged his gaze down neck and across her chest. His reward? An eyeful of cleavage. A fringe of lace revealed the black of her bra as her shirt shifted aside.

He sucked in a breath and glanced up when her fingers dug into his ass.

Their eyes met.

Primal desire flooded Levi's system. Raw and undiluted, it instantly drowned out the shallow thrill he'd been flirting with. She stared up at him, eyes dark and pupils huge, lips parted as she fought to breathe—she was as caught up in the moment as he was.

He stopped moving, could only stare down at her.

And no matter how long he lived, he'd never forget what she did next.

Harper pulled her hands from his pants, grasped the free material around his thighs and yanked, divesting him of his rip-away pants.

The crowd went absolutely insane.

Breath still coming rapidly, she managed a shaky smile. "Your move, Mr. Walsh."

"Since you've just divested me of my pants in public, why don't you call me Levi."

Her chin tipped up as she laughed. Truly laughed.

Levi shivered.

But he couldn't lose focus. He had a responsibility to the men working for him, now truly *his* employees. Then there were his parents. He'd do almost anything to ensure his friends' safety, but for his parents? There was nothing, *nothing*, he wouldn't do to make sure they were never destitute again.

It was time he stopped following where Harper directed him and instead started leading her where he needed her to go.

5

HARPER'S HEART HAMMERED against her rib cage, threatening to break free and gallop off. The night wasn't supposed to have gone down like this. She'd been fine until she touched him. That had set off all kinds of warnings that turned her nerves to live electrical wires. Little shocks skittered across her skin every time he moved her hands, and then there were his hips. He was doing things that were physically impossible. She was sure of it.

She yanked her hands away, but he caught them and slid her fingertips over his nipples.

She sucked in every ounce of air her lungs could hold. She caught the smell of his cologne, the faint hint of fabric softener and the musk of heated skin.

Sensory. Overload.

A hard shiver racked her body.

He paused and shifted to gaze over his shoulder. "Holding up okay?"

"Get on with it," she hissed.

"Remember you asked for it, Investigator Banks."

"What? No! I—" She didn't get the rest of her denial out. There wasn't an opportunity to reply before Levi spun, bent low to wrap his arms around her thighs and lift. He handled her as though she was a five-pound bag of sugar.

Slowly and with absolute control, he slid her down the front of his body, stopping when they were nearly groin to groin.

"Arms around my neck." The words were soft, the command undeniable. Both were meant only for her.

Caught up in the moment, her arms went around his neck.

"Legs around my waist."

"I don't think so." She started to pull her arms free and he leaned forward, forcing her to hold on if she didn't want to be dropped. Her legs went around his waist almost instinctively. *That sneaky bastard.*

Straightening, he began to pump his hips, bumping an undeniable erection against the seam of her sex. Arousal burned hotter than a flash fire—whipping around them, fast and out of control. A whimper escaped her. Whatever he'd been playing at earlier, he was now strong, demanding, in control. All of those things hit every button labeled Desire she had. She'd never wanted to submit to anyone, but he made her crave his brand of dominance in the strangest way.

His lips brushed the shell of her ear when he said, "You feel amazing, Investigator."

Investigator. Reality ripped through her with a viciousness she couldn't ignore. This man was part of her investigation. He'd lied to her already. So, no matter what she wanted in this moment, he was totally off-limits. Period.

She struggled in his embrace.

Levi shifted so he was standing, knees bent, with her thighs resting on his, and pinned her legs behind his back by parking his elbows on his knees.

She was effectively trapped. "Put me down, Mr. Walsh."

"Oh, I don't think so. As they say, the show must go

on." He ground against her, hitting her clit with practiced precision. She jerked then scowled at him, and he laughed. "Such a sour look on such a pretty face. Why do you try so hard to hide your beauty, Investigator Banks?"

Stiffening, she forced him to readjust his hold. "Shut up, Walsh, and let me off this damn stage."

His eyelids slipped low as he considered her. Moving to the center of the stage, he set her down with a soft command to stay still.

Her only movement was to habitually tug at her sleeves.

The music's bass thumped across the air, vibrating through her only to settle firmly between her thighs.

Levi stalked around her in an ever-widening circle until he was standing in profile near the front of the stage. With a flourish, he dropped to the stage and did one-armed push-ups with apparent ease. The muscles in his arm, his shoulders and his back flexed, tightened and moved under the hot stage lights.

She couldn't stop staring as the crowd screamed for more.

He went to all fours and crawled along the edge of the stage, women positively raining money down on him. Waistband full of cash, he glanced over at her and grinned wickedly. He was on his feet in a blink and striding toward her, dropping to his hands and knees when he was halfway there. He crawled the rest of the way, the muscles along his shoulders and down each side of his spine rolling with the motion in the most delicious way. Stage lights shone off the sheen of sweat that decorated his bare skin. His gaze was absolutely predatory.

Harper shivered. She'd never been looked at like that, as if she was the ultimate prize. Awareness thrummed along her nerves and made her skin too tight all over her frame. The way her clothes rubbed and touched made her squirm. She wanted to run, wanted to stand still, to stay and see what this sexually charged man might do.

And that—that wanting—was what totally kicked her out of the moment. She couldn't afford to want. Wanting came with both personal and professional costs, and those costs were way too high. Backing away from him, she shook her head and turned, searching the stage wings for a way out.

There. To the right an exit sign glowed red in the dim corridor. She strode toward it with the absolute conviction that if she didn't reach that door, she was going to become the proverbial fly in this spider's web.

No. No way. Never again.

Marcus had taught her all about being caught up in the moment and what it could ultimately cost. He'd used her, clean and clear. He'd made sure she was busy modeling while he funneled the money from their custom motorcycle shop to his private offshore account. She was the one who had busted her tail only to end up busted-ass broke in the end. If Levi thought he could play that card, if he assumed he could sway her from her sworn duty just by looking at her with such promise, he had another thing coming.

Fighting not to run, she made it to the door before a hot, hard hand closed over her upper arm. "You're not leaving, are you? You still have work to do tonight."

She glanced over her shoulder at the tall man with the executive haircut and green eyes. "Do I know you?"

He jerked his chin toward the stage where Levi was cleaning up, taking ones and fives from the crazed fans. Stagehands were sweeping up money. He seemed to have done very well, perhaps better than normal. It would be worth sticking around to observe his reporting practices on that kind of income. It was, after all, why she was here. It had nothing to do with watching an unnaturally attractive man take his clothes off. Nope.

"I'll ask again," she said quietly. "Do I know you?"

"Name's Eric Reeves, though my stage name is Dalton Chase." He stared at her, eyes cool and gaze professionally detached. "I dance."

She looked him over, taking in his fireman costume. "That's easier to buy than the building being on fire."

He snorted.

The music faded out at the same time the DJ's voice flooded the room to announce the next dancer—Dalton Chase.

"You're up," she murmured.

Eric nodded, took two steps and stopped. He rolled his ax back and forth on his shoulder and didn't turn around when he said, "Watch your step."

Crossing her arms under her breasts, she considered him for a brief moment. "Courtesy or warning?"

"Yes." And then, in the space of a single heartbeat, his whole persona changed—his shoulders squared, a dimpled smile appeared, his eyes were alight with flirtation and the promise of fun.

Surprise made her clumsy as she stumbled into someone. "Sorry," she murmured, regaining her balance.

"You're welcome in my personal space anytime… Investigator."

Spine rigid, she spun and glared at Levi. "What were you doing, dragging me onstage and then getting a little bump and grind going?" She hated that her voice shook. It wasn't much, but he would certainly notice.

He did. "You weren't completely averse to it, so stop acting as if it bothered you."

That was exactly the problem. It *had* bothered her, but not the way he assumed.

"I'm here to observe your reporting practices," she sputtered, stomach lodged in her throat. "Now. And please put some clothes on."

"I'd prefer to shower and get dressed. You can either wait for me, or we can go over the books with me like this." He swept a hand down his body like a *Price Is Right* showgirl offering up the prize package.

She couldn't help but picture him in the shower, wet, soapy, head tilted back under the spray. "I want you... Take me...now..." She trailed off, eyes locked on his pecs.

"Yeah?" His voice was low and smooth, like heated dipping chocolate.

Looking up, she whispered, "Yeah."

He stepped in close. "Feeling's entirely mutual."

She finger-walked her hand up his chest, weaving her hand through his hair and feathering her finger through his waves. "Is that so?"

"We are *absolutely* on the same page," Levi breathed, running his hand from her wrist to her shoulder and down her side to rest at her waist. He lowered his face toward hers.

The moment their lips touched, she smiled. "Excellent. Then we're both interested in getting to the books as fast...as...possible."

He froze, their lips barely touching. "Books?"

She arched a brow, never breaking eye contact. "I don't *think* I misled you, did I? I was under the impression we both understood why I was here tonight."

Levi swallowed loud enough she heard him over the general noise. "I'm disappointed that's where you want me to take you, but I'm sure we can work something out." With a wink, he put distance between them and started down the hall, bare butt cheeks flexing with every step.

Admittedly enjoying herself, she followed the man down the hallway toward the light. Every step was a personal struggle, a battle almost, to keep her eyes off that taut ass in front of her.

In the end, if it had been a true battle, she'd have flown the white flag of defeat without regret.

The view was totally worth it.

LEVI KEPT HIS stride long, his movements brisk enough to force Harper to jog at times to keep up. It wasn't the kindest thing for him to do, considering the stilettos she sported, but he was frazzled. Seeing her tonight, a dark-haired bombshell who dripped sexuality one minute and then seemed uncomfortable with it the next? It made him curious about her story, because the one thing he'd learned between this business and a hell of a lot of pillow talk was that everyone had a story. That curiosity often got him in trouble, though rarely with women. He never had problems keeping his interest in check regarding the women who passed through his life, and Harper *was* passing through.

He still wanted to know why she was so off and on, hot and cold, though. What kind of damage would it take to make a woman who looked like her, who clearly had her mental game together, so unsure of herself? He hated un-solved puzzles, despised unsolved mysteries. He needed to fix whatever was screwed up in the club and then move on, and that meant he had to figure out what made Harper Banks tick.

"What is this place, a freaking maze?"

He glanced over his shoulder, watching her as she picked her way through a pile of cables that were used for Nick's silk ribbon acrobatics show. Ingrained manners had him offering her a hand.

She stared at him.

"Fine. Do it yourself, but don't break an ankle in those heels."

"I can manage the heels."

He intentionally picked up his pace, moving toward the break room the guys used between sets to eat, lift weights and just shoot the breeze. Pushing through the swinging door, he found four guys inside. Two of them were filling out their state and federal tip-reporting forms.

Please let them be doing it right, he silently pleaded to whoever might be listening.

Every eye shifted his way, took him in and then came to a full stop when they noticed the woman behind him.

"Ethan, Mica, Trey, Justin—this is Harper Banks. She…" He stumbled there, unsure how much to tell the employees. Sure, Justin knew, but it was easier for Levi to share this particular burden with him and Eric. With the guys like Ethan, who worked this job after-hours to pay for his wife's fertility treatments? Or Mica, who depended on stripping as his sole source of income while he went to school? Or Trey, who'd ended up here when his unemployment ran out and he had no other options but still had to feed his kids? These guys didn't need the added burden the IRS brought with it, brought with *her*. No, they deserved a little peace while Levi figured out what the hell had happened and, more importantly, how to salvage the business.

"Looks like the introductions failed at hello," Harper murmured. Stepping around him, she approached the men, all in various stages of undress, and shook each hand with professionalism and calm control. "I'm Harper Banks. I'm going to be looking into Beaux Hommes's business practices over the next few days. Bear with me as I ask questions and try to learn as much as I can about the club."

"You the new part owner the front office was chattering about?" Trey asked, eyeing Harper with open interest.

"New part owner?" She faced Levi and arched a brow.

"Hey, I'm just a dancer." First the declaration he didn't work in the office at all, then the ledger duck and now this, lie number three. This totally wasn't his speed. He'd always been much more a take-it-on-the-chin man, not a lie-to-cover-your-assets kind of guy.

She considered him carefully before speaking to the group again. "Anyone know who this new part owner is?"

The scattershot reply garnered a general no, though Levi noticed Justin didn't answer. Instead, the other man kept working on repairing the zipper on his surfer costume.

Harper's gaze settled on Justin. She must have noticed he hadn't responded. Of course she noticed. She noticed everything and everyone.

"You didn't answer."

The other man considered her carefully before he spoke. "The front office doesn't share a lot with us beyond very generic gossip, changes to personnel policies, paycheck pickup times—that kind of stuff. So, no, they haven't told us who the new part owner is."

She crossed her arms under her breasts. "You want to share the general gossip?"

"I'm not into gossip."

Harper leaned a hip against the table Justin worked from. "Who is?"

He looked up. "Probably none of the dancers."

"Pretty tight group, then."

Justin shrugged and went back to working on his costume. "If you don't mind, I have to get this thing fixed before my set and it's being a real pain in the..." He glanced up at her pointedly and lifted one shoulder in an absent shrug. "Well, you know."

Levi had to fight the urge not to punch his best friend in the face for the dig even as he swallowed his laughter. She knew. Oh, yeah. She knew.

But it bothered Levi that the other man was being rude to Harper. Which was stupid. She was in here asking these guys to turn on the company that helped them pay their bills and feed their families. If she thought she had a hope in hell of getting any dirt out of them, she was going to end up sorely disappointed before the week was out. And it was already Thursday.

There was an audible snap and Justin grinned. "Got it!" Standing, he yanked his sweats down to reveal a tiny G-string with a fishing bobber on the end of the—

"Dude. I told you to drop the ornaments on your junk," Levi said on a sigh.

"Yeah, well, how else am I supposed to be sure I've got a bite?" he asked, grinning.

"Someone bites your junk, you're *sure*," Mica said emphatically before blushing. "Begging your pardon, ma'am."

Harper grinned at him. "I can't imagine having your junk being turned into a snack pack is any fun."

"Snack pack," Ethan said, choking on a laugh. He finished filling out his tip-reporting form and stuck it in an envelope. He scribbled his name on it, time-stamped the corner and carried it to a mail slot near the door. He deposited his tips and with a nod said, "Nice to meet you, ma'am," then left the room.

Justin finished shimmying into the wet suit and zipped it up as he, too, headed for the door. He paused long enough to splash some water on his hair and run his hands through it, affecting a true surfer look. Grabbing his beat-up surfboard, he grinned at Levi in an almost feral way. "Twenty says black coffee."

Levi's lips twitched. "Not making that bet, my man."

"Thirty."

"Not a chance in hell."

"Fifty. It's my best and final offer." When Levi hesitated, Justin grinned. "Gotcha. Besides, you might as well take it. You know I'm going to ask, anyway." Blinking slowly at Harper, he shifted into his stage persona, giving her a slight bow. "Be good to our man here."

"Guys, you want to clear the room for me?" Levi asked. The others silently rose and headed out, Levi's thanks resonating as they left. He flopped into an empty chair at the table and waved Harper into the opposite one. "So, ask away."

She eyed him strangely. "First, what was Justin betting with you on?"

"It was a joke. Let it go."

"I'm curious."

"And I'm not explaining it. It has nothing to do with this investigation, so let it go." *Lie number four.*

Harper sank into her seat with control and grace. "Fine. How about you let me start with those time cards and tip sheets. We can go from there."

With a crisp nod, Levi rose, grabbed his keys out of his locker and went into the adjoining room, gathered the envelopes and returned to the table. "The envelopes fall into a mail basket, where they're collected the following morning by the front office staff. The office staff member scans each envelope's face into the employee's electronic records before counting the take and logging it in the payroll system. Hourly wages are calculated, the tips are reported and paychecks are issued at the end of each week. The file is submitted to the government electronically when payroll is done and, to the best of my knowledge, the IRS hasn't ever had a problem with our reporting practices."

"You're very familiar with how the office is run, Mr. Walsh."

He slid down in his seat a bit, crossing his arms over his chest. "Yeah? Well, aren't you familiar with your job? Do you know how things like the IRS's payroll system works?" He grinned when she just sat there. "See? You figure out what's going on around you if it's important enough. This?" He gestured around the room. "This is important enough to me that I want to know how it runs."

She stood and paced away, giving him a clear shot of her tight ass.

He wanted to tell her she was beautiful. If he did, though, she'd likely bite his head off. Instead, he asked, "Why do you keep your sleeves down? It's hot as hell in the club, but you kept them down out there as well as earlier in the office."

"Dress code," she murmured.

And wasn't that a kick to the gut, the reminder that she was on the clock and not here because she wanted to be. None of this was about the chemistry that burned up the air between them. That reality chapped his bare ass. He'd just have to make a more concerted effort to change her mind.

A smile tugged at one corner of his mouth.

His thoughts snapped back to Justin's bet. *"Twenty says black coffee."* He'd been betting that Levi would end up making Harper coffee tomorrow morning, that he'd take her to bed tonight and make her another one of his conquests.

He wouldn't. Harper was a different breed of woman, one who didn't play lightly. When she got involved, Levi imagined it was for keeps.

And he wasn't the man for that job.

6

HARPER'S EYES BURNED. It was 3:00 a.m. She'd been over every tip-reporting form in the bin, and each one had been filled out correctly. There were minor math errors that the front office should catch when they audited the forms prior to submitting them. That was no big deal. And she had to assume the tip totals were reported correctly, because she hadn't been there to see the men count their cash takes down. She despised assumptions, but to follow the cash from the moment it came off the stage to the point the men turned it in would mean another trip to the club. She wasn't sure she despised assumptions that much.

Sighing softly, she chanced a quick glance at Levi. She'd insisted he take a shower and get dressed about two hours ago. He'd been gone less than twenty minutes and, not for the first time, she envied men the ability to get themselves together so quickly. He'd looked refreshed and delicious, even when he put his glasses on and got down to business—*especially* when he put his glasses on and got down to business. He was smarter than she'd initially given him credit for. That surprised her. *He* surprised her. Everything about him was a mixed message, from his appearance to the way he covered up his intelligence with smart-ass remarks to the clear way he hid behind his glasses when he was offstage. She wanted to understand him, his motivations and…

Stop it.

He'd lied to her. She knew it, and there was no circumstance that warranted a blatant, in-your-face, outright lie. That was simply a hard and fast rule of hers, and *as* it was her rule, she'd be following it to a T.

Standing, she locked her hands behind her neck and stretched, arching her back until her spine felt as if it would snap apart like children's building blocks. Her muscles shook with the release and she relaxed, shoulders slumping, chin to her chest.

"Long night for you, I suppose." Levi's voice bridged the distance between them, a tentative thread of compassionate connection.

"Longer than most, but only because I've been up since I caught the red-eye. The time change seems to have teamed up with jet lag in an attempt to knock me out."

"Particularly lethal combination, that." He stood and mirrored her stretch before pulling her chair out. "Have a seat."

She didn't try to hide her suspicion when she eyed him.

"I'm not going to assault you, Harper," he said on a sigh. "Just have a seat."

Muscles tight with everything from exhaustion to mistrust, she slipped into the chair. His hands gently rested on her shoulders for a moment before sliding up to her neck. His thumbs dug into the muscles at the base of her skull and she groaned out loud. As he alternated deep massage and soft touches, Harper found herself moving wherever Levi encouraged her to go.

When he leaned her forward and slid his hands lower down her back, she wordlessly propped her forearms on her knees and went with it.

His hands roamed down her sides, fingertips tracing her ribs as his thumbs worked the muscles along her spine. "You're incredibly tense." The soft timbre of his voice fit the moment.

She let her chin dip lower as he moved up to her shoulders again. "Goes with the job, I guess."

"Can I ask you something?" When she tensed, he softened his touch. "You don't have to answer. I'm just curious."

"If I don't answer, you won't press?" Sounded too good to be true.

"On my honor."

"Then by all means, ask away." It bothered her that she could hear the stiffness in her answer, but she couldn't unsay it, couldn't make it sound smoother and less rigid.

The minutes passed, and all he did was rub her shoulders. Just when she was about to literally shrug his touch off and get up, he spoke.

"Why did you join the IRS?"

Air rushed out of her on a long exhale. How to answer? So many options to choose from, ranging from the bare bones to the complicated truth. Rolling through the possibilities, nothing sounded right. Instead, she asked, "Why did you become a dancer?"

His breath whispered over her neck when he chuffed out a short laugh. "You first, Harper. I'll answer you to the same level you answer me."

Fighting the feeling she'd been cornered, she forced her hands to hang loose between her knees. "I wanted a job where I could stop companies from running over their employees, from being dishonest and practicing thievery in the light of day under the guise of ethical business practices."

"Sounds personal," he observed quietly.

"It was. Is." She shrugged. "Some days I wonder how

much I do the job for others and how much I do it to prove to myself I'm not so gullible anymore."

His hands slowed. "Gullible how?"

"Same old stuff that landed me here, I suppose—falling for the things I want to hear, failing to see what's right in front of my face because I want it to be something other than what it is." Her laugh hung somewhere between self-deprecating and bitter. "Typical stuff."

"*Your* definition of typical, maybe." He played with the ends of her hair, tugging and twisting. "As promised, though, I won't push for more than that."

Harper fought off the urge to purr. His hands were warm and soothing, *too* soothing. "Stripper story."

"I'll give you as much as you gave me." Sliding his fingertips through her hair, he began massaging the pressure points on her skull, his touch almost absent. "I was in college, a fresh twenty-one and was a little awkward in social situations."

She snorted. "I can't imagine you being awkward."

"Hush. This is my story."

"Fair." Harper shifted slightly under his touch to give him better access.

"I wanted into a particular fraternity, and they said I had to try out for a stripper gig with a couple of other newbs. A few girls from their favorite sorority came along to make sure we showed up." He laughed, little more than a whoosh of air. "I not only made it into the fraternity, but I got a job I very much needed at that point."

"Why?" she pressed.

"I had my own financial responsibilities. And it was pretty cool to go from being the odd man out one day to being wanted by hundreds of women the next." He cupped her neck, thumbs absently stroking the base of her skull. "We should probably call it a night."

She turned in her chair, considering him. "Fair enough. I'm still curious about why you needed the job."

"And I'm curious about what it is you wanted to hear so badly, what you wanted to believe in so badly, that you'd allow yourself to be led astray. Doesn't mix with the woman I know."

Facing him now, she met his steady gaze. "But that's just it. You *don't* know me. Not really."

His hands fell away from the bare skin of her neck, the lack of contact severing the intimacy of the moment. "Very true." He stepped away, hooking his thumbs in his pockets and watching her with undeniable interest. "Want to pick this up again tomorrow?"

Flushing unexpectedly at the intensity of his gaze, she gathered up her paperwork, copies of the tip-reporting forms and her notes, shoved them in her messenger bag and swung it over her shoulder. "I'll see myself out."

"I'll walk you to your car."

"I'm good."

He stepped ahead of her and opened the door. "I insist."

"And I decline your offer," she said, soft but firm. "I've lived alone long enough to manage doorways and chairs and, surprisingly, even more complicated things like folding bottom sheets and finding a decent plumber."

"Bottom sheets, huh? Impressive." He yanked the door open and waited for her to pass through. When she stopped, he scowled at her. "I bow to your superiority. Now go through the damn door."

"You first."

"You know, I'm a huge proponent of female independence and equality. But when a woman turns down a courteous offer, I'm of the opinion the idea of independence is taken too far." Muscles knotted at the base of his jaw and gave her a sick sense of satisfaction. "Go. Through."

"What do you mean I'm taking it too far? If I don't want

to have my doors opened, my chairs pulled out or whatever, that's my choice."

"I'm going to stand here until you walk through this door, and if I get tired of waiting, I'll haul you out myself."

She sputtered but backed up a step. "I don't think so, Clark."

"Clark?"

"Kent. You know—Clark Kent. He puts the glasses on and he's one person and he takes them off and he's another." Heat rose up her neck and slipped across her cheeks. Her propensity to tell the truth when flustered was one of her biggest personality flaws.

He chuckled, the sound cooling the temper between them. "Just go through the door, Lois."

With a long-suffering sigh, she stalked outside and kept going, heading for her car. "Happy?" she called over her shoulder.

"Beside myself with glee," he answered drily.

She shook her head with disgust.

Light reflecting off metal caught her eye. Nearly stumbling to a stop, her mouth gaped and her eyes nearly bugged out of her head. Her heart beat hard enough to rattle her rib cage. Dropping her belongings to the ground, she stepped over to the motorcycle. Her hands itched to trace the bike's lines but stopped mere inches from the surface with a kind of reverence. "This is a 2010 Harley Dina Wide Glide. It's all about the rumble with this one. Low-slung bodywork makes turning an arc versus an angle, but this baby is meant to show off a little, and what better way to do it than to take curves with a little arrogant grace?" She held out a hand, hovering over the red-flecked black metallic paint, the flames on the fuel tank seeming to dance and flicker a few shades lighter in the streetlight. This bike had been a dream of hers from the first time she'd seen it. She spun around. "Is it yours?"

"If I said yes?"

"I'd beg for the keys. I'd plead. Hell, I'd let you open all the doors for me you wanted without a single word of complaint." She was actually light-headed. That this bike was right here in front of her made her want to scream. She did a little hip shimmy and dropped down, balancing on the balls of her feet as she checked out the chrome work. "Whoever did the paint and shine did a good job. You hire someone?"

"Yeah."

His soft, almost inaudible response made her glance back. "What?"

"Nothing. You want the keys?" He rattled them. "I'm assuming that, considering you're bike crazed, you have your motorcycle license."

"I've been riding since I was old enough to reach the handlebars on my electric Power Wheels." She paused, biting her lip. There had to be a catch. "What do you want in exchange?"

"Kiss me good-night."

She shot to her feet, every hair on her body rising in a fight-or-flight response. Lips numb, she fought to form a response. "I'm sorry, what?"

Levi blinked slowly. "You heard me." He flipped the keys on his pointer finger around and around, the *swish-clink* noise mesmerizing her. "It's a simple trade, Harper. You drive my bike, I get a kiss."

"I...I..."

Scooping up her belongings, he nodded toward the car. "Open the trunk so I can dump this stuff before I rupture something. What the hell do you carry with you—your entire workstation?"

He moved to the rear of the car and waited as she dug the keys out of her pocket.

He was so confident she'd capitulate. So sure of himself. "I can't."

"Can't open the car?" he teased.

"Can't—" she swallowed so hard it hurt "—kiss you." Still, she beeped the trunk open.

Levi dumped her belongings inside and slammed the lid. Pivoting, he leaned a hip against the car's rear-quarter panel and crossed his arms. "Sending mixed messages, there, Ms. Banks."

"I won't jeopardize my job. I *can't*." Though the response was meant to be firm, it came out with an air of longing she regretted, would've given anything to take back. "I can't, Levi. I'm…sorry." And that was the hell of it.

She really was.

LEVI SHOVED HIS hands in his pockets and jangled his loose change. "We'll see."

Harper stalked to the car, yanked the door open and settled into the driver's seat, but didn't close the door behind her. "You always this arrogant?"

"Nope. I usually save it up for special occasions." He'd affected the lazy drawl to rile her. It worked.

"And I assume this is one of those times?" she snapped.

"Definitely." And that was the truth. He liked to be in control, but he pushed hard enough to come off as arrogant. She just happened to hit the right combination in him to bring out both his best and worst traits at once. Like lying.

It pissed him off that he'd been painted into a corner, forced to defend himself and those around him via any means, be they fair or foul. But the IRS was predictably overbearing in its tactics. He'd seen what the agency could, and would, do. He'd been in the front row when it had auctioned off his family's stuff. He'd tried to buy back what he could. But without sufficient wealth at the time—the

kind of wealth the IRS both understood and respected—
he'd been able to reclaim very little.

And now here he stood, flirting with his declared nem-
esis and *enjoying* himself. The reality almost choked him.
If someone had named him traitor to his family right then,
he wouldn't have contested it. His stomach did a lazy roll,
the kind that shoved his lungs out of the way and made it
hard to breathe.

And yet his strategy of distracting her by keeping her
on edge was working—she hadn't asked again for the ledger he'd promised to give her. So for the sake of his family
and friends, he'd continue this charade.

Shoving off the car, he stalked toward his bike, singling
out the key on his key chain as he went.

The car door slammed behind him at the same time he
threw his leg over the bike's seat and shoved the key in
the ignition.

Click. Click. Click-click-click.

He heard muffled cursing, and he glanced over his
shoulder.

Click-click-click-click. A heavy *clunk* resonated across
the still night. Stilettos slammed onto the asphalt, sounding
like tiny gunshots, as Harper stalked to the front of the car
and hoisted the hood, mumbling to herself. She reached
into the car and paused, judiciously ignoring him. "Damn
it," she said on a breath.

"Car trouble?"

"Nope. I'm in here looking for D. B. Cooper."

"Huh. I've never heard the theory he ended up under a
midsize economy car's hood."

"Causing trouble wherever he goes," she muttered.

Even edgy as he was, Levi laughed.

Harper faced him, wiping her hands on her jeans.
"Don't suppose you have any tools around here, do you?"

"Eric's the one who'd have tools on him. His little car's always crapping out on him."

"Great." She ran one hand through her hair, smudging grease—grime?—on her forehead. "Does he live close enough to call?"

"He has to get up in about three hours for his day job, so calling him is out." Levi considered her. "You seem confident you can fix it yourself."

She snorted, one corner of her mouth curling up in a heart-stopping smile. "Sweetheart, with a few tools and a twenty-four-hour parts store? There's not a compression motor out there that I can't fix."

"Now who's arrogant?"

"Not arrogance if it's fact." She paused, assessing. "I'm not ruining this shirt." A heavy sigh escaped. "What the hell. I'm off the clock."

His brows drew together. "I'm not sure which statement to respond to."

"None of them. Just…do me a favor and don't mention this to anyone."

"The car breaking down?" He was confused. "Because I'm not pursuing the kiss."

"The kiss was never even up for debate." She shot him a quick, weighted look. "Don't mention I rolled my sleeves up around anyone involved in the investigation." Fingers at the wrist cuff, she hesitated. "I'd appreciate it."

"What the hell are you talking about?" he demanded.

Shaking her head, she unbuttoned her shirt at the wrist and began to roll one of the sleeves up. She revealed solid ink sleeves—colorful, beautifully done tattoos.

Waves around the wrist were marked with fish and starfish. A little farther up her arm, the water faded into sand. That changed into solid, rugged turf with profiled evergreens framed by the night sky. The blue grew darker and, from the very edge of the sleeve, he saw the lower crescent of what he assumed was the moon.

The other arm was a complementary pattern, but it was all done in daytime colors, with the sun peeking out from under the rolled-up shirtsleeve.

Whoever had done the work was seriously gifted. Details kept surprising him—a bird here, a shell on the shore, the way the tip of the tree bent in the invisible wind. It was magnificent.

"This is absolute art. Why keep it hidden?" He reached out to touch a mountain drawn across her bicep, and she flinched.

"Dress code. No body ink or piercings, besides the ears, can be visible."

"Yeah, but your office is in Washington, DC. No one would know—"

"Those are the rules," she insisted, pulling out of his reach. "Breaking them gains me nothing."

"And you don't do anything unless it's for personal gain?" *What kind of life is that?*

"I don't do anything that might hurt me." Her eyes flared and she took a step back.

Levi realized she must have revealed something too intimate. *But what?* Nothing she'd said was wildly unexpected. "Harper, I—"

"Stop," she said, interrupting. "Just stop right there. I don't want this to be personal, Levi. I don't want this to *become* personal. It'll only hurt worse when I shut Beaux Hommes down. I won't have my judgment questioned or my ethics compromised by a handsome face and a great body." She crossed her arms under her breasts and tucked her chin against her chest, shoulders heaving.

"Nothing personal, huh?" Irrational as it was, the idea pissed him off. "Okay. Fine. Nothing personal. But you're not going to close us down, Harper. Beaux Hommes has been built on the backs of the men who perform here, and you won't take that away from them. Are we clear?"

She slowly lifted her face. Her eyes were flat in the glare of the streetlight. "I don't want to take anything away from them. I want to stop management and the owners from participating in illegal activities that could cost these guys their jobs or worse. It's the owners I'm after. Not the dancers or the other staff. Clear enough for you?"

He swallowed audibly. "What if you find something the owners didn't know about?"

"Then they should've been more diligent. There's a certain amount of culpability that comes with ownership. You don't just hand the reins over to someone and blindly allow them to run the company. That's sloppy business."

And that was exactly what Beaux Hommes's owners had done. The three men he knew, the men who had convinced him to buy in, had trusted Kevin with everything. Hell, *Levi* had trusted Kevin.

He needed Kevin to freaking show up and explain himself.

Harper shivered and started to roll her sleeves down. "It's too dark to see and too late to do anything about this tonight. Anything you want to tell me before I go, Levi?"

"Yeah."

She paused, waiting.

"You're going to get your sleeves dirty if you intend to work on your car."

She gave a small shake of her head. "I'll call a cab tonight and the rental company in the morning, but thanks for your concern."

As angry as he was about Harper threatening to shut the club down, he didn't want the night to end on a sour note. She'd never trust him enough to break the rules if he didn't manage this better. He took a deep breath and cleared his throat. "I'll give you a ride back to your place."

"Thanks, but a cab would be easier."

"I'll let you drive." She looked up at him, eyes wide, and he dangled the key well within range of her hand. "C'mon."

She reached for the key only to pull her hand back at the last second.

"Are you always so suspicious?" Levi's pointed question came out brisk, borderline harsh and obviously annoyed.

"People don't perform random acts of kindness for the IRS, Levi."

"Maybe they'd be more so inclined if the IRS practiced random acts of basic human empathy before they set out to destroy someone's life," he bit out.

Harper jerked as if slapped. "I told you—that's not what I'm here to do."

"Look—" Levi ran his free hand through his hair "—you asked why I dance. I have a history with the IRS. Not me, exactly, but my parents. They were screwed by the system." His voice hardened, and he tugged at his collar. "They aren't criminals, Harper. They were third-generation farmers that Mother Nature crapped all over."

She started to respond but he shoved a hand between them, palm out in the stop gesture. "Don't. Do *not* apologize."

"But—"

"I mean it, Harper. Don't. You have no right to come in here with same intent as they guys who robbed my parents and then turn around and offer empty words of condolence for everything we lost. It'll only piss me off more." Truth was, he was already pissed off—because he knew Harper just well enough to know her condolences would have been sincere. If she didn't mean it, she didn't say it. Shaking his head to clear the thickening emotional haze, he waved absently at the bike. "You want a ride back to your place or are you going to call a cab?"

She considered him as she refastened her shirt's French cuffs. "I want to drive."

"Make it a polite question." His low prompt was an undeniable command.

"How about I throw in a *please*?"

He arched a brow.

Clutching her hands to her chest, she lifted her face to his, wide eyes nearly glowing with sincerity. "May I take you up on your highly magnanimous offer to allow me to drive this mechanical Goliath, the one that forcefully thaws the edges of my oh-so-frigid heart with a passion heretofore unknown?"

"Cute." Reaching up, Levi dragged a hand across his mouth to hide the unwilling smile that threatened.

But then the reality of the situation hit him. He had a sudden mental image of himself straddling her hips as she drove, his hands resting on her waist...or higher... or *lower*...

He tossed her the keys. "That'll do."

She snatched them out of the air and shot him a sardonic stare, but she didn't start for the bike until he stood at its side. Then she worked the parking lot like a catwalk, eyes pinned to the motorcycle, completely oblivious to the way his tongue nearly rolled out in a cartoonlike gesture. She might be IRS, but sweet heavens, she was *hot*.

Desire reared its head, and he breathed in the air in an attempt to catch a whiff of her.

Watching her move the way she did, seeing her make love to the machine with her eyes then trace her fingertips over the glossy paint equated to total seduction. *His*. And when she swung a leg over the leather seat and his cock gave what could only be called a happy little shimmy, it made him realize he was in far deeper shit than he'd realized.

He might despise the IRS. He might hate why Harper

had been sent to Seattle. He might wholly resent the power she wielded from the moment she'd walked through the door. But he was going to thoroughly enjoy getting under this woman's skin. His body reacted to the thought, transmitting its feelings on the matter. Apparently his mind and body were in accord.

The sooner he got his hands on her, the better.

7

HARPER TRIED FOR calm when Levi casually flung a leg over the pillion, settled his feet on the foot pegs and rested large hands on her waist. The flutter in her belly said she failed. With his chest pressed against her back, he offered undeniable warmth. She fumbled the gearshift—second to third—and the bike lugged. Downshifting, she caught second again and shot forward, fishtailing a little.

Levi's alarmed shout made her grin. Obviously he had no faith in her. She wanted to ride dirty, but this wasn't the machine for it. Too bad. She probably could've taught her passenger a thing or two.

Let him learn on his own.

She hadn't been lying when she'd told him she didn't want this to become personal. When he'd told her about his parents, though, it had crossed that invisible line and become just that. What they'd experienced couldn't have been easy on anyone in the family, let alone the—oldest? youngest? only?—son. But right now she had a bigger issue.

Levi made her feel feminine and alive. His personal challenge perked up all her competitive instincts. But the fact he made her *feel* was ultimately the worst. It gave him a certain influence over her, piquing her slightly neurotic compulsion to make sense out of chaos. He was an enigma. He'd lied to her, but she was beginning to understand that his deception was motivated by his incomparable sense of loyalty—and that fascinated her. It also made him more dangerous than anyone else she knew. Infatuated people made stupid decisions. Her own history provided all the proof she'd ever need of that.

Turning onto the on-ramp, she accelerated, hitting the interstate at speed.

Levi's hands gripped her hips more firmly, and he settled his groin against her ass. Before she could object to the general proximity of the guy's package, he slid his fingers inside the front pockets of her jeans and curled them into the supersensitive soft spot just in front of her hipbones.

"Hands off, Levi."

"I have to hang on to something. At the moment, you're my only option."

Fighting to stay calm, to not make more of this than it was, she shifted slightly. The bike was heavy enough it didn't even bobble. And damn that man if he didn't follow her every move.

Leaning into her, he fused his torso to hers, eliminating any space between them. The heat of his chest radiated through her thin jacket. The tip of his nose skimmed the shell of her ear when he rested his chin on her shoulder, face—and particularly lips—canted toward her. "Everything okay?"

She barely heard his question over the montage of the traffic, the wind and the hammering of her heart. "Respect the driver," she snapped, leaning forward enough to create the illusion of personal space.

Again, he mimicked her move, closing the distance between them. "You handle the bike like a pro." This time his lips skimmed her ear.

"Like I said, I've been handling these things nearly all

my life." The whip of wind carried her words away so she couldn't be sure he'd heard her.

His response assured her he had. "And what is it about bikes that intrigues you so?"

She tensed.

"Harper?"

He'd obviously felt her reaction, and she couldn't blame him for being curious. But she had no intention of providing an answer. Besides, even if she wanted to respond, she didn't know what she could say that would make sense to him.

I learned to dream over machines like this. My dad taught me to dream, and dream big. He instilled in me the core value that you never settle for good enough if you're given the chance to do something better...or right.

"Talk to me." Levi followed the command with a sharp squeeze to her hips and a short thrust of his own.

Battered as she was by the wind, she couldn't catch her breath, couldn't find the air necessary to respond.

"Harper?"

"I'm not sure how to get back to my hotel," she shouted.

He pulled his hands from her pockets. Relief proved both premature and short-lived when he settled them at her waist, his thumbs tracing the slight sway of her lower back, over and over. After what seemed an eternity, he lifted one hand and cupped it around the front of her neck, nestling her against his chest as he reached with the other hand to help her steady the bike. "Tell me where you're staying."

The intimacy of the gesture sent her mind and emotions reeling like a pair of drunken square dancers. Everything seemed out of tune, offbeat and just generally wrong. Her mind spun. Grasping the first thing her mind pitched her way, she said, "Make it a question."

His laugher rumbled through his chest and reverberated

up and down her torso. "Fair play, Banks. Tell me, where are you staying?"

A hard shiver ran through her. "That's splitting hairs."

"Proper inflection made it a legit question."

"The Hilton downtown."

He let her go with no more warning than he'd given her when he'd touched her. "Take the Madison Street exit. Stay in the middle lane and stay to the left."

She nodded, shifting forward on the seat as she edged the throttle up. His thighs tightened around her hips and she suddenly seemed small within his hold, petite even, caught in his strong grip.

Danger zone, Banks.

He made her crave a night of pleasure, one that would leave them both satisfied but still able to part ways at dawn.

She took the third exit as directed, caught the green light and rolled through the corner.

Levi leaned with her. "Take a right on Fourth Avenue, then left on Sixth. Hotel will be on your right." Slipping his hands along the outside of her thighs, he brought them to rest with his fingertips tucked under her legs. His thumbs rested in the crease between her mons and upper thighs.

"Hands!"

"They're good, thanks."

The obvious smile in his voice made her want to elbow him in the ribs, hard. If she ditched the bike, the road rash would be worth it.

But there was a risk. What if her colleagues saw the accident report in the paper? They could accuse her of indiscretion and get her thrown of the case. No way would she hand the jerks in her office more ammo than they already had.

"Call uncle and I'll move my hands."

"I'm more likely to call the dead sled to come pick up your body after I strangle you with the brake cable."

He tightened his grip and pressed his groin forward.

Harper tried not to gasp at the rigid length of him pressed intimately against her ass. "Levi!" It annoyed her that his name on her lips was filled with equal measures of irritation and arousal.

"I've developed a real appreciation for riding the p-pad tonight." He breathed against her ear. "Besides, I gave you an out if you really wanted it."

"Uncle." But she little more than mouthed it, certain he wouldn't hear her. It shamed her she was so hungry for the intimacy of his touch that she couldn't utter the one word that would put an end to his teasing. And that's all this was. Teasing.

Following his directions, she took the final corner. The Hilton's sign glowed against the cloud cover descending over the city. A soft rain began to fall as she pulled up under the porte cochere. Sucked he'd have to drive home in the rain, but she wasn't inviting him up to her room to wait out the weather.

Dropping the kickstand, she eased the bike down and shut it off. "She's a beautiful machine," she murmured, slipping from the saddle. His hands lingered on her waist before he let go. "I'll admit I envy that you have her."

Levi slid into the driver's seat. "You handled her well."

She shrugged and forced herself to look away from the distinct planes and angles of his face. "Comes with experience."

"Or it's a gift." He turned the key in the ignition, the rumble of the bike echoing off the porte cochere's roof. His sheer strength proved an undeniable advantage when he pushed the bike to standing and heeled the kickstand into place.

She opened her mouth to respond to the compliment, but he revved the motor and drowned out whatever she might have come up with. "Asshole," she mouthed. Then she leaned into his personal space, ignoring the way his eyes flared with heat, and shouted, "Next time, keep your damn hands to yourself!"

He grinned, revealing deep smile lines. "No." It would have been irritating if it hadn't been so boyishly endearing.

Endearing.

God, she really was going to have to watch herself around Levi.

"Endearing, my ass," she muttered, stalking toward the door held open by the doorman.

He had touched her, not only physically and not exactly emotionally, but there had been more than one moment tonight when she'd experienced a basic connection with him. For the first time in her government career, a suspect had blurred her line between personal and professional. And she had no idea how to push him back onto the appropriate side. He was charming, funny, surprisingly intelligent and, yes, endearing. And she wanted him.

She paused and looked back over her shoulder, watched as the Harley wove through downtown traffic until its taillights disappeared.

With a shuddering breath, she turned back to the doorway.

Then she remembered. She spun around again, glaring in the direction Levi had gone.

After all the flirting, the long hours at the club, the tentative connection, the way he'd touched her—that jackass hadn't given her the ledger. Heat spread up her neck and across her cheeks.

He'd kept Harper too distracted to notice.

That stopped now.

FRIDAY MORNING CAME far too early for Levi, who typically went to bed in the a.m. and rose in the p.m. Today, though, he was up and at the small desk in his compact apartment before seven. He was sure Harper would be digging around as soon as she got a new rental car and someone opened the office for her. Levi needed to work through at least part of Kevin's ledger before he met with her today.

Cursing more creatively, he downed the last of his luke-warm coffee before pouring a fresh cup. He was honest to a fault most of the time, but the livelihoods of more than one family rested on the decisions he made now. If anyone had told him six weeks ago he'd be lying his ass off to cover for the club, he'd have laughed. Now? Oily guilt rolled around his belly, protesting the coffee he sipped.

He dug Kevin's ledger out of his messenger bag and carried the worn book to the table. His laptop was already open, a clean Excel spreadsheet waiting for him, cursor blinking in the first blank cell on the page. Patting his head, he found his glasses and pulled them down to bring the screen into sharper focus.

The only way he knew to get this mess cleared up was to make sense of the ledger. Unscrewing the binder's hinges, he pulled the scratched-up pages out and numbered them before putting the book back together so only fresh paper remained. He opened the ledger he'd reviewed prior to investing in the club and settled in to begin reconciling the two.

"Once more unto the breach," he murmured, clicking his adding machine on.

It was slow going. Nothing made sense. Some entries were blotted out with correction tape and written over, while Kevin seemed to have simply scrawled over others repeatedly. The original numbers were indecipherable. Worse? Very little between the two journals matched.

"Oh, come *on*," Levi nearly shouted when he saw that only two weeks ago Kevin had listed payroll as income. And the dollar figure recorded was roughly five grand higher than the two pay periods prior.

Grabbing his cell, he dialed Kevin's number. The call went directly to voice mail.

Thumbing the screen off, Levi tossed the phone to the table. He was going to murder Kevin because it was now clear that the ledger in his hands was evidence of fraud. But why? The club seemed profitable. Why cook the books?

His phone buzzed, vibrating across the tabletop and displaying a number he didn't recognize. Snatching the phone up, he swiped the screen to answer. "Hello?"

"Mr. Walsh."

That voice. "Good morning, Ms. Banks. I'm discouraged we've reverted to such formal address, and before nine a.m. at that."

"Cut the crap, Walsh. You promised me the ledger if I upheld my end of the bargain. I did. You, however, did not. I'm giving you sixty minutes to produce it before I get a warrant for your arrest."

"I apologize, Harper. Honestly."

"Use that word very carefully with me." Her words were slow, her tone unbending.

"What word?" he demanded, pacing the length of his kitchen.

She paused. "Any form of the word 'honest.'"

Levi's stomach plummeted. How much could she suspect in twenty-four hours on-site? He swallowed audibly. "I'm well aware of the word's definition and its appropriate use."

"Duly noted."

Background noises from the harbor and the interstate registered. "Where are you?"

"I'm sitting in the office parking lot."

"Why don't you go in, get a cup of—"

"The office isn't open."

Levi stumbled to a stop. "The receptionist should've

opened the office—" he glanced at the clock "—an hour ago."

"Place is locked up tight, lights out, no cars outside besides mine."

The need to pound his fist into something made his hands ache. Damn Kevin! Clearly he had known something was going down and chosen to disappear instead of manning up. "Give me thirty minutes."

"You have any idea why the owners aren't answering their phones?" Her question was laced with cool curiosity.

"Not a clue." He ran a hand around the back of his neck and pulled, trying to ignore the fact that, as an owner, he'd answered his. "I'll try and get them on the line."

"I'll see you in thirty, then." The disconnect was silent. No click. No buzzing line. She was simply gone.

Tossing his phone on the table again, he pulled his T-shirt off and headed for the shower. He had to form a plan before he got to the office. Because Kevin and maybe even the other owners had set the dancers up to pay for their crimes. And Levi would be the first one forced to settle the bill.

8

HARPER LEANED AGAINST her replacement rental car and tipped her face to the sun. The deep blue sky formed a brilliant stage for the white-and-gray gulls that circled and cried, diving down to steal bits of bread and such from each other when the children fed them. Traffic hummed in the distance, the occasional horn disrupting the city's white noise. She could totally get used to this place. Washington, DC, was a cacophony of sound, shouts and threats.

Gravel crunched as a generously tuned black Camaro pulled into the lot and parked. Levi unfolded himself from the car, slamming and locking the door. He started for the front entrance without looking at her. "How long have you been out here?"

Her watch read straight up ten o'clock. "Since eight thirty. Where's the bike?"

He shrugged. "Felt like taking the car today."

"I was under the impression you'd be here thirty minutes ago."

The muscles at the back of his jaw knotted. "Had to make a few calls."

She jogged across the uneven asphalt. "What's going on here, Mr. Walsh?"

His hesitated, the key inches from the front door's lock. Instead of answering her, he shifted to lean a shoulder against the door and look her over. "If I told you I truly don't know?"

"I'd be forced to consider whether or not you were covering for someone." She shrugged when his brows shot up. "Honesty isn't going to hurt either of us as much as lying will."

He shoved off the door and jabbed the key in the deadbolt. "And how are you so sure I'm lying?"

Oh, I know your lies all too well. "It's my PBD."

Pulling the door open, he gestured for her to enter first. "PBD?"

"Professional bullshit detector. It's a honed weapon in the right hands."

His laughter seemed to echo through the empty office. "And yours are the right hands?"

She didn't answer, just followed him inside.

He clicked on the lights and moved through the desks to fire up one of the printers. "I seem to recall you requested a dedicated printer. What else can I get you?"

"The ledger would be a good place to start." Tension raced across her shoulders when he hesitated. "You have one opportunity here, Levi. The law won't allow me to keep you out of jail if you impede this investigation. You understand that, right?"

A terse nod was his only answer.

They stared at each other across the chasm of different priorities.

"I want to propose a solution," he said, voice low and strained.

She blinked slowly. "I agreed to negotiate with you once. That was mistake enough."

"I can help you figure out what's going on."

"So, what, you're going to go undercover and snoop?

This isn't a Scooby-and-the-gang investigation," she said caustically.

"No, it's not. It's an IRS investigation that has the real potential to shut down the club and force financial hardship on a lot of people I care about. I can't stand by and let that happen. Let me help you figure this out."

"It's against the rules."

"And you're an absolute rule follower." he stated, stepping forward. "Please, Harper. Show a little compassion here."

There was a factor here he was avoiding, and she wasn't about to go out on a thin limb in a stiff wind without a thorough understanding of exactly what that factor was. "What's in it for you?"

"I can't afford to lose my job, either."

She might have bought it, but he'd hesitated just a fraction. *More lies or, at the very best, partial truths.* "And why is that?"

He visibly stiffened, his lips thinning and eyes going hard. "You're already aware of my parents' situation. Delving any further into my personal life is out of bounds."

"Is it?" She crossed her arms under her breasts and cocked her head to the side, considering him. "Only seconds ago you were appealing to my compassion, and just last night you wanted to make this personal."

All the color leeched from Levi's face. "You want personal?" he asked, the strain in his words making them brittle. "Fine. What do you most want to know? What it felt like to watch the IRS auction off my great-grandmother's wedding quilt for twenty bucks? Or maybe you're more interested in what happened after my parents were essentially turned out on the street. What makes this personal *enough* for you, Harper?"

Words wouldn't squeeze around the knot in her throat. "They would have had options, payment plans—"

"You think my old man was ditching taxes because he didn't *want* to pay them? He couldn't, Harper. Big difference. Huge."

The anger that radiated off him made her fidgety and slightly anxious. Feeling her way forward with caution, she said, "I sympathize with your parents. A lot of people in farming and ranching get the short end of the stick due to inheritance laws and such, but that's outside my realm of expertise. I deal with tax evasion and fraud. Period."

His mouth opened and closed several times as he searched for something to say.

She pressed on. "I wouldn't wish that on them, Levi, and I wish I could change that for you and your parents, but the law is the law. I have to uphold it."

"I wish I could have changed it for them, too. I couldn't help them when it happened. I was a kid, in college." He tunneled his fingers through his hair and gripped his skull hard enough to make his biceps flex. "So let me help these guys. I'm pretty good with numbers."

"Pretty good won't cut it where this is—"

"Don't judge me because I dance."

Shaking her head, she tried not to remember his *dance*. "I appreciate the offer. I do," she stressed when he started to object. "I just don't know what you can do for me that I can't do for myself."

He considered her, his brows drawing together. "Do you always have to do everything alone?"

The question hit so close to her emotional epicenter that her stomach pitched. Still, she answered him honestly. "Pretty much."

"That's a lonely way to live," he said quietly.

"It's safer." The words were out before she could weigh and measure their potential impact.

He nodded. "Like I said, lonely."

"Look, Levi—"

"I can get you copies of the bank statements."

Her fists clenched. "You're already obligated to produce those."

"Just let me help, Harper. Let me make a difference in the lives of these men when I couldn't save my parents' legacy. They lost everything through no fault of their own. I don't want to see that happen all over again to more people who mean something to me."

The impassioned words struck a nerve. Wasn't that why she said she'd gone into this job?

What if someone had taken that much interest in her dad's employees when it was clear the shop was going under? Would someone have been able to turn things around? She might have been that person if she'd been brave enough. And if she'd been brave enough, she would have fought back when Marcus had walked out on her and left her to bear the brunt of the IRS's scrutiny. Harper knew just what she'd be doing to these people if she shut the club down. The idea didn't sit well with her.

"I can't accept investigative help from outside the department. It's against—"

"—the rules. I know. But sometimes the rules that are there to protect people do just the opposite. I'll get you into all the files. I'll make sure you have unfettered access to the business accounts. Just let me try to help solve the problem before you shut the business down and put a lot of people out of work."

She blew out a deep breath.

He stepped forward, closing the distance between them, stopping close enough that the heat his body gave off soaked into her skin. "Let me help. Please."

The tension that radiated across her shoulders spread through her back and down her arms. "You'll hand over everything."

"I will."

Her eye twitched. "I could force you to do that, anyway."

"Yes."

The simple admission swayed her. "You could cost me my job."

He arched a brow. "Pot, kettle."

"I want this case closed within the week."

"Then let me help."

"You're going to support me in stopping whatever's going on here."

"If it's illegal, yes."

It was the most she could ask for if she wanted to close this case on her own. Like a repeat of last night's soundtrack, she remembered her dad telling her never to settle for good enough if she could be better. This was her chance. Was she brave enough to take it?

She held out a hand.

Levi took it.

She gave a terse nod as they shook on the silent agreement. "Let's start with the bank statements."

LEVI FOUGHT NOT to punch a fist in the air and shout. He'd persuaded her. He had a chance to stop his friends and family from suffering. This was his chance to make it right. He was *not* going to blow it.

She stared at him so skeptically he couldn't help but laugh. "You look like I'm going to try to dismantle the organization you hold so dear."

"No. I just…"

"What?"

"Nothing. Forget it." Rooting around in her messenger bag, she pulled out a laptop, legal pad and a pen. "Pull together a list of everyone employed by Beaux Hommes—names, dates of birth, Social Security numbers. Then I want the tip-reporting records, the ledger, all of it. While I review those, you can start copying bank records." She paused. "Don't make me regret this, Levi." She pulled out the desk chair and started setting up her equipment, adding her computer to the club's wireless network as Levi watched.

Opening his messenger bag, he pulled out the ledger he'd been given by the owners—the one that had seemed legit to him. "I'll grab the files and log in to the personnel system to generate that list."

Her gaze skipped to the ledger. Resting her hand on it, she nodded once before returning her attention to her computer screen.

Levi strode down the hall to the file room, pulled out his keys and unlocked the door. What he found inside stopped him in his tracks.

File drawers hung open, their contents clearly having been rifled through. Paper littered the floor. One filing cabinet lay on its side, its drawers ejected and the contents spilled all over the place. Locks on the drawers hadn't been pried open, though. No, whoever had been here had had a key.

Levi's stomach cramped hard enough to have black spots dancing across his vision. How much did he tell Harper? She'd want that list of employees, would want to see their corresponding files.

There was no way he could clean this up without her wondering why he'd disappeared. She'd come looking for him, and when she found him with this mess? It would be easy to assume he'd been trying to get certain paperwork disposed of before she could get her hands on it.

He'd have to show her.

Sighing, he stepped farther into the room and let the door go. But the resounding thump that should have announced its closure never sounded. He looked over his shoulder to find Harper holding the door open, her eyes trained on the mess.

"What's going on?" she asked as casually as if she'd asked if he took cream and sugar with his coffee.

"Why do you assume I know? You'd have heard me if I made this kind of mess," he snapped. "Besides, I haven't been gone long enough."

"I'm a field agent. I'm trained to pick up hard-to-spot clues like that." She stepped inside and let the door close before sinking to the balls of her feet and picking through some of the paperwork. "Did you come back here last night?"

"No." The answer was ripped out of his throat and issued through clenched teeth.

"Does this place have an alarm?"

Fighting to control his breathing, he nodded.

"Does everyone have their own code to get in?"

"No. There's one code for everyone."

She considered him, eyes guarded. "Who has access to that code?"

"Management, office staff, owners. I don't know who else." Muscles in his shoulders and neck knotted with admirable efficiency as a tension headache settled in like a squatter.

"I'll need to take a few pictures of this and then get into the security system to see who came in and when. You keyed the alarm off today, so any fingerprints are going to be lost."

Except mine. She didn't say it, but she didn't have to. The accusation hung between them. He wanted to defend himself, but it wouldn't do any good. The more he tried to explain he was innocent, the guiltier he'd look. Talk about a rock and freaking hard place.

She stepped out, advising him to not touch anything, and returned moments later with a small digital camera. "Which files are stored in here?"

"Everything that isn't public access, I think." He

glanced around, the sinking sensation in the pit of his stomach gaining momentum. She started systematically sorting through files. "I want to get what's here boxed up and itemized."

Stepping around her, he grabbed a flat banker's box and began assembling it. "Shouldn't you call for...I don't know...backup?"

She ignored the question. Slapping a lid on the first box, she hoisted it onto her hip. "After you box this up, I'd appreciate it if you'd bring it to me and then get me that employee list."

"Sure." He silently began gathering files, stacking them in alphabetical order as his mind wandered over the little bit of information he had about her investigation and just what kind of trouble he was in. She'd said her division was tax fraud and evasion. That covered a lot of possible ground. The charges could be anything from failing to pay quarterly employment taxes to not paying any taxes at all. Or there could be criminal dealings.

And the person he suspected was the real criminal—Kevin—was MIA. Levi was the last person to have talked to the guy since yesterday morning, and when Levi called the other owners after Kevin's disappearance, none of them copped to having seem Kevin in days. It was then, as a group, the other owners had been unanimous in their decision to have Levi handle the IRS investigation. Regardless of the fact he was the team's newest member, he was also the financial expert among them. Levi had suggested handing the case over to their accounting firm, but no one was entirely sure who that was anymore. Kevin had claimed to have hired a "better" firm months ago. Seemed he hadn't passed that piece of information along after the change. Given the way things were developing, Levi was willing to bet there was no firm. Otherwise Kevin wouldn't have been able to run the books the way he had. That meant Kevin was dirty. How dirty, though, Levi couldn't tell.

Hauling the next box of files out to the main office, he considered what he knew about Kevin. The guy was undeniably bright, but decidedly aloof. Levi had always taken that for professional distance, but suddenly it held a much more distinct flair that leaned toward consciously removed. Everything he knew about the guy seemed suspicious now that Levi had cause to doubt him. It was disturbing.

He continued to pack and haul until the file room was empty. Depositing the last box on the floor near Harper, Levi sank into an office chair. "That's all of it."

Harper had begun to create spreadsheets, written ledgers, notes and more with brutal efficiency. He admired the way her mind worked in such an organized fashion. Shifting in her chair, she absently kicked her shoes off and adjusted her skirt so she could tuck one leg up under her butt, reminding him he found more just her mind attractive. His gaze lazily ate up the length of leg she'd revealed. He took in the slight swell of her hips and nipped waist before pausing to admire the way her breasts pushed against the fabric of what he already considered her trademark long-sleeved shirt. Knowing the shirt hid those magnificent tattoos was like having a wicked, highly coveted secret.

Levi continued his perusal. The slope of her shoulders led to her neck's graceful curve and up into the thick black cap of hair he suddenly wanted to run his fingers through. She was remarkable.

Shifting to relieve pressure on his swelling cock, he found he wanted to tell her what he saw when he looked at her. Yet the guarded way she dealt with people, particularly him, warned him to exercise caution. She'd been kind to the guys last night, asking questions and even bantering with them a bit before the club closed. It had touched him. Still, she'd remained tense and very protective of her personal space. He'd been aware of this, yet he'd still pushed her boundaries when they'd driven to her hotel. That hadn't been kind of him at all. He'd been curious, though. Her wariness had wordlessly shouted that her personal story was far more complicated than anything his imagination might conjure, but her confidence declared she didn't bow to history's influences. It made her an enigma, a puzzle to sort out.

Focus, Walsh. You need a puzzle? Get back to the ledger. There's more at stake here than figuring out what makes her tick.

Levi pressed the heels of his hands to his temples. Obviously exhaustion had reduced his mind to engine sludge. He had to pull it together. His obligation to the club and his fierce determination to protect his parents superseded his passing attraction. And that's all this was—a passing attraction. He had no intention of settling down, let alone with a woman who worked for the IRS and lived in DC.

He started when she spoke. "Where would I get files on the owners? I want to verify the information I have and fill in the blanks for the stuff I'm missing."

His testicles retreated hard and fast before lurching to a stop somewhere near his liver and making him twitch. Hard.

She pulled her glasses off. "Levi?"

Forcing himself to relax his grip on the chair's armrests, he met her gaze and shrugged. "I don't know where they keep all the incorporation files, but what you need is probably in there."

That much, at least, was true.

9

By Sunday night, Harper wanted nothing more than to grab a six-pack of beer, retreat to her hotel room and grab a long, hot bath. Everything ached, from the soles of her feet to the tips of her hair. It figured. She'd been running flat-out since she got off the plane, and she needed a break. But even after four days, she was nowhere near close to closing the case.

Levi had done whatever she'd asked without complaint—and without touching her. He'd worked diligently to translate the ledger into an Excel spreadsheet as well as digitize files. Every morning he'd pass her a thumb drive with the compilation of his efforts. She'd download it and return it to him so he could repeat the process the next day. But she was running out of time to solve this case on her own.

Tonight they were doing inventory on the bar. Watching him, she had to wonder if he was sleeping at all. Dark circles ringed his eyes like bruises. His skin had taken on an unhealthy pallor, and his hands shook slightly when he passed the clipboard she asked for.

Setting it down on an empty shelf in the alcohol closet, she propped her forearms on the shelf's edge and considered him. "Are you okay?"

His chin whipped up. He blinked rapidly. "I'm fine."

She arched a brow and blatantly eyed him. "You don't look fine."

Eyes glittering, he set down the bar code scanner and crossed his arms over his chest. "Would you like me to grab a costume from the locker room? Do a little 'inventory'—" he made exaggerated air quotes "—in assless chaps to make things more interesting, perhaps?"

"Pricked a sore spot, did I?"

His feral grin made the angles of his face appear sharper. "So the queen of spreadsheets has a temper, does she?"

"Just as much as the assless-chaps master does," she bit back.

Levi's grin faded. "Think so little of me, do you?"

"I never said—" She stopped when a door in the club slammed.

"What the—"

Harper slapped her hand over his mouth and hissed, "Quiet." Moving to the door, she reached out and eased it nearly shut and turned out the light. The room went black as pitch save for the sliver of glowing red from an exit sign nearby. "Where's the egress for this room?" she whispered.

"It's a bar. Building code doesn't require us to have one for interior rooms designated as storage."

Voices registered, deep enough to declare them male and sharp enough to determine they belonged to some seriously pissed-off men.

"—or I'll cap your ass and deal with the damn consequences!" one of them shouted.

Harper reached for her weapon. It wasn't at her hip. "Shit," she breathed.

"What?"

Levi's voice was so close she jumped, her heart lodging in her throat. "My gun's in my messenger bag."

"Where'd you leave the bag?" His hot breath washed over her ear.

Shivers raced up her spine, spreading through her hairline even as heated embarrassment chased across her cheeks. "Cabinet beneath the printer."

"What kind of federal agent stashes her weapon?"

"The kind who's never had to fire it before in the line of duty." She faced Levi and, with absolute control, reached out and fisted Levi's shirt. "Who knows we're here?"

He answered swiftly—*too* swiftly. "No one."

"Liar," she breathed, and tightened her hold when he stiffened.

Silence hung between them, heavier in the darkness as the voices grew closer, raised in irritation.

Harper listened as she pulled her smartphone off the clip at her waistband. Shifting to put her body between the screen and the door, she lit it up, switched the ringer off and opened her camera app. She kept her hand cupped over the screen and slipped closer to the door. Then she hit record.

For several seconds, the voices were so muffled she was sure the phone wouldn't pick up anything. She pressed even closer to the narrow space between the door and the frame, holding the microphone toward the conversation.

The men moved into the main club area, and suddenly their raised voices were clear.

"You don't have to threaten me. I'm telling you, Mr. Wheaton, I got rid of the cotton, beans and tango."

"And *I'm* telling *you*, Kevin, that the good doctor has volunteered to castrate you *without* the benefits of Rohypnol if you screwed this up, too. You're lucky he didn't euthanize you when you farked up the ledger transfer," Wheaton grumbled. "I should've just shot you."

The first man, apparently the missing club manager, Kevin, moved closer to the storage room. Oddly he sounded more anxious about the threat to his balls than he had to being shot. "I didn't screw up! I got the rest of the stuff out before she got here. She isn't going to find anything. Everything else is cooked."

Footsteps sounded in the hallway outside.

Harper eased the door closed.

Levi clamped a hand over her mouth while his free arm banded her arms tight to her torso. He yanked her in to his body and lifted, dangling her feet several inches off the floor.

Panic swept through her. What if she'd misjudged him? What if he'd been working to get her here late at night, alone?

She struggled against him, trying to decide if making noise might gain her an advantage.

He took the decision away from her when he laid his lips next to her ear and nipped her lobe to get her attention. Breathing hard, his whispered command was harsh. "Stop." When she failed to comply, he tightened his arm around her body so that she could hardly breathe. "I'm moving us into the corner. You'll go face-first, I'll press against your back. My jeans, T-shirt and hair are dark."

She startled when he lifted her farther off the floor and moved them into the corner.

"Stay. Still," he ordered, dropping his hand when she nodded. Settling his body tightly against hers, he ran a hand down her arm only to pause at her wrist. "Give me your phone."

"Why—"

"Now."

Fighting the urge to argue, she handed it over at the same time the security code was entered into the keypad. The electronic lock whirred, then the door swung open and the light flashed on.

Facing the corner, she couldn't see who had come in.

She listened instead as the man muttered, quietly cursing the owners.

Kevin. It had to be Kevin.

Something solid landed on the shelf before he began moving bottles, the clink of glass inordinately loud. Metal scraped metal as he moved things around on the shelf. Hinges squeaked. Plastic rustled as Kevin dug through what she assumed was a box. "Ought to charge them more for redistributing this crap."

Kevin shoved the box back across the shelf with a hair-raising screech, and more bottles clinked sharply as he re-placed them. The door opened, the lights went out and the heavy lock latched with a hum.

A third voice, more muffled due to the closed door, joined the others. "Walsh's car is parked out back alongside a rental car."

Levi stiffened against her.

The statement was met with silence. Then the first man, Wheaton, shouted, "Levi! Get your ass out here!"

"Don't," she breathed. She hadn't meant to speak, but the fear he'd expose them drove her to issue the plea aloud. A range of emotions—fear, hope, desperation and more—weighted that one word.

In answer, he wrapped his arms around her and pulled her in to his body. "They don't get either of us. Not without a fight."

She relaxed into his embrace, for the first time wholly confident that Levi was telling the truth.

LEVI HELD HARPER closer as she slowly relaxed. It totally shook him, the amount of faith she'd placed in him. Almost as much as the emotional plea she'd issued—*"Don't"*— had leveled him without fair warning. He had no intent of announcing his presence, not unless it meant preventing Harper's discovery. And if that happened, if things went that sideways, he needed to ensure what little evidence they had was preserved.

Taking her cell, he used the light from the face to quietly move a handful of bar supplies around so the phone was hidden but the microphone on the bottom pointed out. He left it recording. If they were discovered, he wanted the whole thing documented. Surely someone would find it. And if they made it out? She'd have everything she needed, and more, to close the club down. At this point? He knew he'd have to live with that.

Levi had begun to seriously wonder what kind of game the other owners and Kevin had been playing. After hearing that short conversation between Wheaton and Kevin, he now knew.

Cotton, beans and tango were the street names for the prescription drugs OxyContin, Adderall and fentanyl, all of which were heavily controlled substances. Kevin had been using the club as a clearinghouse and distribution point, but Levi doubted the guy was bright enough to orchestrate something this big. That meant the other owners—one of whom was, conveniently, a doctor—were probably involved.

Then there was Levi. *Why had they been so keen for him to buy in? Had they wanted to pull him into their drug business? Or had they intended him to be the fall guy all along?* He had no clue, but it didn't matter. His name was on the partnership. Bile rushed up his throat at the realization the feds would only see him as a coconspirator, not a victim.

"Walsh!" the third man shouted.

The truth had leveled Levi so effectively he didn't even startle at the sound of his name.

"Probably banging the woman in the locker room," Wheaton said, laughing. "Guy's a total whore."

"You think he's switched sides?" Kevin asked, voice tight.

The third man answered. "He's got as much to lose as the rest of us. So, no. I doubt the man's anybody's Judas."

Levi's fingers dug into Harper's arms. She objected with a small jerk, and he forced himself to relax his grip.

She wiggled free, stepping away to put distance between them. He stopped her before she got far. "If you run into something and make a noise, we're marked. Hang tight, okay?" Swallowing hard, he added the most questionable of commands. "Trust me."

The men outside lowered their voices to hushed whispers.

Harper moved to face him, settling into the loose embrace of his arms and speaking against his chest. "Something's not right. They've gone too quiet."

"No doubt." Levi strained to listen, shifting them closer to the door. He'd recognized the third man's voice. It belonged to Mike Lazarus, a real estate magnate and one of the owners of Beaux Hommes. *How far did this mess go?*

Levi could still hear the men's voices, but they were too low to understand. Whatever it was they were discussing, he doubted it would bode well for him and Harper.

Absolute silence descended between heartbeats. No more low-level discussion. No more movement.

"If you're here, Walsh, come out. We're done screwing around." Mike's shouted command made both Levi and Harper jump.

She rested her forehead against his shoulder and shook her head. "I'm not at all on board with waltzing out there."

"Shh." Levi moved her aside so he could press his ear to the door.

Several minutes passed, and Mike called out one last time. "Best of luck to you." The dry sarcasm in his voice made every hair on Levi's body stand up.

Somewhere beyond the hallway a deep, almost metallic *clunk* sounded and, seconds later, a faraway door slammed.

Levi waited but heard nothing else. "I think they're gone. Still, I'd be more comfortable if we hung out here for a bit to make sure they aren't waiting us out."

"Agreed." She was still whispering.

"Stay there for a second."

"Where are you going?" she hissed.

"Nowhere." Her panic surprised him until realization dawned. She was scared he'd bail on her. "I won't leave you, Harper. I give you my word." With short, shuffling steps and eyes closed, Levi worked his way across the room by memory. He'd stocked this room enough to know where everything was. It only took a couple of minutes to find what he was looking for.

Harper's eyes flared when he lit the small votive, set it on a high shelf and blew the match out.

"They're the candles we use on the tables. Should be small enough I doubt they'll see the light under the door even if they're around. Still, we'll keep it back here. That cool?"

She nodded and crossed to him, huddling close to the flame. "We can also move a few of the supply boxes in front of the threshold to block the light."

He smiled. "Smart girl."

Between them they had the door covered well enough that a little light would be safe.

Levi lit a couple more candles. "I've been through this room a hundred times for inventory or to retrieve bar stock. How did I not see something out of order? It sounded like Kevin dragged a box out."

Harper took a votive to the shelf and looked. "If he's hiding it here, it's not in plain sight."

"You don't think he took it with him?"

She shook her head. "He put something back." Moving

bottles as quietly as possible, he watched as she traced her fingers along both the top and bottom sides of the shelves. A grin lit up her face. "Bingo."

A soft click and a lid disguised to match the shape of the shelving popped up to reveal a surprisingly wide and deep box set into the shelf itself.

"I'll be damned," Levi breathed, looking it through. Reaching in, he felt around and retrieved two pills—one round and yellow, the other an oblong orange capsule. "Seems he missed a couple." Pulling out his wallet, he dropped them inside before catching the look on her face. "I'll give them to you when we get out. You don't exactly have anywhere to keep them."

Her mouth tightened. "You'll give them to me?"

"On my honor."

She didn't respond.

He ignored the silence. "So, how long do you think we should hang out?" he asked even as he dug out a few table-cloths and laid them down on the industrial tile floor. Sitting, he patted the ground next to him.

She shrugged. "You know these guys. How serious are they going to be about watching the building?" Kicking her shoes off, she sat and tucked her legs to one side.

Levi swallowed hard. If he'd thought she was beautiful under the office's fluorescent lighting, candlelight rendered her ethereal. "They might put Kevin on it, but I doubt it," he answered, the strain in his voice evident. Running a hand around behind his neck, he pulled until his arm shook. "It's probably best if we give them a couple of hours—maybe three. Unless you want to call the authorities?"

Her sigh made the nearest candle flame flicker and sent shadows dancing along the walls. "We'll wait. I'm not ready to explain why I'm sitting in a candlelit closet with…"

"A suspect," he finished for her. "It's okay, Harper. I get it. For the record, I'll try not to make enduring my presence a hardship." The gentle teasing made her smile.

"You're not."

His brows winged down. "Not trying?"

"Not a hardship," she murmured, eyes downcast before she squared her shoulders and lifted her chin. "You've been a lot of help the last four days."

"Thanks." He closed his eyes. There was quite a bit he should tell Harper, but he didn't know how to begin. Starting with admitting he'd withheld Kevin's working ledger made the most sense, but he couldn't bring himself to say the words.

Instead, he slowly looked up and met her gaze. They had a few hours to kill—might as well get familiar. "If you could have a single do-over in your life, what would it be?"

10

HARPER'S MOUTH FELL OPEN. What did a person say to that particular question? Especially when said question came from someone she was (a) ferociously attracted to and, (b) would probably arrest for fraud, and tax evasion. And when the DEA got wind of this, illegal drug trafficking and distribution would undoubtedly join the charge party.

She hadn't said a word, had fought not to react when she'd heard the street names for the prescription drugs, but she'd recognized them all. Levi hadn't reacted, either. If she'd only been able to see his face, she might have been able to find even an iota of surprise. She didn't want him involved in this, didn't want to find out that the lies he'd told her were only the beginning, the tip of the proverbial iceberg.

She shook her head. She'd been getting to know him over the past four days. She'd watched him manage the dancers who interrupted as she and Levi worked. He'd handled each man with compassionate authority. When one guy had called in at the last minute because his child was sick and his wife was working, Levi had excused himself to work one stage set. No bitching and moaning, he'd just done what needed to be done. When another dancer came to Levi, upset that he'd been salaciously groped by a customer and his G-string had been torn away, Levi had calmed the guy down. Then Levi had gone to the floor and personally escorted the woman from the club with firm instructions to both the woman and security that she wasn't allowed back on Beaux Hommes property. Ever.

So many things pointed to him being a decent, honorable man. Except, of course, the fact he'd lied to her. But she'd begun to understand him through the actions she witnessed. Levi truly was as fiercely loyal, hardworking, loving and faithful as she'd once accused him of pretending to be. And then there was tonight. He'd chosen to stay with her, to put his body between her and the door, to protect her. He must have realized the consequences of sticking around. Had he handed her over, he could have potentially walked away from this. But he hadn't. He'd put her needs before his own. If that type of self-sacrificing behavior didn't tell her she could essentially trust him, nothing would. It would just help if he'd come clean about his involvement in this.

"You going to answer or just sit there staring at me like I'm a fascinating inhabitant of the psych ward?" Words gruff, they failed to disguise his nervousness.

A tentative smile pulled at the corner of her mouth. "You're too tall for a straitjacket. The orderlies would have to tranq you just to manage you. That plus your muscles makes you more a candidate for the gorilla exhibit at the zoo."

His teeth gleamed white in the softly lit room. "You like gorillas?"

"Enough to answer this one's question." She lay down on the tablecloths, surprised when he joined her and wiggled his arm under her head. Her gaze slid sideways to take him in.

He met her eyes for a moment and then shifted to stare

at the ceiling. "The floor's hard and without a pillow, you might pinch something in your neck," he explained.

"Thanks." Further evidence she didn't want that supported her assessment that he was both kind and thoughtful. *Just great.* Sighing, she allowed herself to relax at his side and tried to ignore the fact that his cologne made her want to bury her face in his neck and breathe deep, or that his warmth and sheer size made her want to curl into his side.

Clearing her throat, she forced herself to consider the question. *What to tell him about my mistakes?* The answer seemed so easy. *The truth.* If she wanted him to offer it voluntarily, it only made sense she offer him the same. "There are several things I'd do over. It's hard to choose just one."

"The one most important to you right now."

"I…" She fisted her hands against her belly. "You first."

He glanced at her. "Fair enough." Without a moment's hesitation, he spoke. "I would give anything to change the way we started."

Shock rendered her mute.

Levi rolled his head toward her, a seemingly sad smile pulling at his mouth. "It's true." A shadow passed through his eyes, there then gone. When he visibly steeled himself, she expected his voice to be strong when he spoke. Instead, his words were barely audible. "I lied to you, Harper."

Anger and fear battled relief and hope in a sudden, fierce and bloody skirmish. As if he'd heard her private wish, he was finally going to provide her with the truth she'd sought from day one. "Go on."

Muscles at the rear of his jaw worked, knotting and unknotting as he fought his own demons. Finally, he answered. "I'm the new part owner of the company."

Tension bled out of her swiftly, the dam that had held her emotions at bay opening to let relief chase away distrust. "Why confess to me now?"

"You have a right to know who you're dealing with. I haven't been very proud of my choices, and they were all mine. I'm also embarrassed at how I've behaved, flirting egregiously one minute and then trying to rein myself in the next."

"The mixed signals were definitely confusing." She kept her voice calm, her demeanor calmer. "It was like trying to speak one language with seven different regional dialects."

He chuckled, his chest vibrating against her shoulder. "That's fair." When he stilled, he tipped his chin down to look at her. "What does this mean for me?"

She didn't have an easy answer. "I don't know yet." The ache in her chest made her want to change the subject, but his honesty deserved a truthful response. "You should probably retain an attorney, a *very good* attorney. Soon."

His sigh shuddered through him. "I figured." Keeping his arm under her head, he rolled onto his side. "For what it's worth, I'm sorry."

Her heart stuttered, faltered, then began to hammer hard enough it would have chiseled through her ribs had the organ had sharp points. Fighting to find her voice, she murmured, "For what it's worth, I believe you." And she meant it.

Closing her eyes, she reveled in the deep relief that settled between them. Soft fingertips brushed the fringe of her hair. Shocked, her eyes flared. "What are you doing?"

He grinned deep enough to reveal twin dimples. "I've wondered for days if your hair is as soft and thick as it looked. For the record? It is."

The urge to shoo him away died on her lips. His touch made her want to hum her approval. "Stop it," she finally muttered, but only halfheartedly. "It's hardly appropriate."

"I'm sure there's some rule against it."

The grin in his words made her huff out a short breath.

When he pulled his hand away, she tilted her face toward him but left her eyes closed. "What?"

"I just spilled my guts, laying down a heavy apology on the 'do-over' menu. It's your turn. What would you do over if you could?"

"Can I think about it?"

"Has your life been that hard?" he asked mildly. When she didn't answer, he touched her cheek, tracing a fingertip down her jawline. "I want the first thing that comes to mind, the one thing that leaps into your head when I ask, *If I could do one thing over again, I would...?*"

Her throat tightened and her eyes burned behind closed lids. "I would have been brave enough to take over my dad's business."

Levi stilled. "What happened?"

Crossing her arms under her breasts, she held herself tight. Then she forced herself to meet his direct stare. "He went bankrupt."

They lay quietly together, the only sound the occasional sputtering of a candle or a particularly defined breath.

When Levi spoke, his words were carefully neutral. "I want to ask what happened, but I think you need to decide for yourself how much you share with me. Particularly now."

"Why?"

"So you don't ever look back at this moment and accuse me of manipulating you in the moment."

There he went again, letting the good guy hidden inside peek out of that bad-boy exterior. She sighed, trying to ignore the way his every word dismantled the walls she'd worked so hard to build to keep people at a distance. It was the only way she could protect herself from the heartbreak of betrayal. Yet he'd earned truth from her, and she'd give him nothing less. "My dad owned a custom bike shop and was always waiting to be discovered as the next big thing. He thought if he worked hard, did right by people and offered quality products, he'd get his big break. He truly believed it would put him on magazine covers and give him the recognition that, to him, would translate to huge financial success. It never happened. He started letting guys go one at a time until he was the only one left. He closed the shop two years after I graduated from college and Mom went to work at a local grocery store to help make ends meet."

Levi tucked Harper closer. "My mom ended up at a big-box store. It's hard to see your old man lose something he's worked so hard for, isn't it. Harder still to see your mom have to bust her ass to help clean up the mess that's left over."

Both of their fathers had lost the very things they'd strived to keep, the things that had meant more to them than anything else. Their businesses had been different, yet, to each man, equally important. And both of their mothers had ended up working the only jobs they could find in order to help pick up the pieces.

Harper couldn't help but wonder about Levi's childhood, if it had mirrored hers or been so different as to be unrecognizable. *Had he given up his own dreams when his father's had fallen apart? Had he wanted something more, but been folded into an uncomfortable mold to make money? Had he been so desperate to prove himself that he'd trusted the wrong people and been proven a fool?*

The questions continued to form, picking up speed. "Did you want to someday take over the farm from your dad?"

Levi gave a short nod. "Yeah. At the time, I couldn't see myself doing anything else."

"So you let the dream go," she pressed.

"After the foreclosure, I suppose I did," he said quietly. "I could've bought another farm, but it wouldn't have been the same."

She nodded. "Right. I get that." Then the question that had dogged her for years slipped out before she could stop it. "Do you think it was easier to decide to let that dream go than to try again, start over, and…maybe…get stuck watching it die all over again?"

Sliding the arm under her head just far enough he could prop himself on his elbow, he looked down at her. Flickering light made his hair glint like obsidian in the darkness. "I made the best choice for me at the time, changed my life goals and found new dreams that had been waiting in the wings, so I never regretted my choices." He cupped her cheek, his eyes roaming over her face. "No one should ever have to watch their own dreams die. Ever, Harper."

Every ounce of air that had been locked in her lungs rushed out when her eyes met his. She had a split second to wonder if her pupils were as dilated as his.

Then he kissed her.

LEVI DIDN'T THINK about the implications, frustrations or potential complications. He simply closed the distance between them and did the one thing that truly felt right. He kissed Harper Banks.

Her lips were full and firm. They parted on a shaky inhale, and Levi pressed the unexpected advantage. Nibbling her lower lip, he ran his free hand around her waist, pulling her in tight against his body. Need raced through him unchecked when her tongue tentatively touched his, an unspoken question If he burned any hotter, he'd prove that spontaneous combustion could, indeed, be caused by sexual desire. Heat from her body scorched his skin. His fingers dug into her lower back as he encouraged her even closer. Short, harsh breaths were like sexual white noise—he heard them, his and hers, and paid them no mind.

She tasted like coffee and smelled like expensive perfume. The combination smothered whatever common sense had been fighting to hold a spot near his conscious mind. Now? Now all he could see was her, think was her, hear was her, smell…was her. And the body under his hands? Man, it was her. *All* her.

The kiss deepened, growing equally in mutual demands and primal desperation. Gripping her skirt, he wiggled it up enough to get a knee between her thighs.

She gasped.

His cock swelled in a rush of desire. He'd never wanted a woman as desperately as he wanted Harper, not even when he'd been divested of his virginity at nineteen by his college roommate's older sister. That had rocked his world. This? Just this kiss had reversed the polarity in his universe, turning up to down, left to right and in to out. He wanted more from her and, at the same time, wasn't willing to stop the kiss to go after it. She was everything to him in that moment. The thought terrified him enough to make him slow down.

Harper pulled away from Levi, covering her mouth with her hand as she made a small sound of distress.

He captured her hand, pulled it from her kiss- swollen lips and pressed her palm over his thundering heart. There were probably a hundred things he could've said, but none seemed adequate for the moment. All he could manage was to stare at her and blink stupidly before shifting his gaze away.

"What?" she demanded, voice hoarse. When he didn't respond immediately, she wiggled out of his grasp and, shimmying and tugging one-handed, forced her skirt into position while the fingers of her other hand fluttered over her lips again. "Why?"

"Why?" he repeated, focusing on her in his peripheral view.

"I didn't stutter," she whispered.

"Is it so hard to fathom I might actually be interested in you?" Her eyes widened, and he pressed on. "Truth, Harper. You'll get nothing but truth from me anymore. I screwed up before. I own the choice and the consequence. But I try to learn from my mistakes and not make the same ones twice." He swallowed hard, the sound obnoxious in the quiet room. "I prefer to mix it up so my mistakes are fresh, never stale. And now I'm babbling. Throw me a bone, Harp."

Her brows winged down. "Do you smell smoke?"

His mind stumbled over the question. "Huh?"

"Smoke." She turned toward the door. "As in, fire."

He shook his head to clear the battering confusion. "No."

Dropping to her knees and shifting boxes aside, she muttered, "Smoke rises. You should be able to smell it before I do."

"Nothing's burning in here except three votive candles. They wouldn't smoke enough to smell unless we blew them out, so—" *Smoke.* He smelled it now, caught a faint curl as it drifted under the door. Harper reached for the door handle and he nearly knocked her down to stop her. "If there's a fire out there, the door could be hot enough to burn you."

Wide gray eyes focused on him. "I'd rather burn a spot on my hand than all the rest of me."

Ignoring her disturbingly sound logic, he grabbed the door handle. He couldn't stifle the resulting yelp.

"You don't have to be Yoda to figure out 'Hot handle, fire there is.'"

He shot her a sardonic look. "Hand me one of those bar towels."

She grabbed one off the shelf and tossed it his way.

Snatching it out of the air, he wrapped it around his hand

and tried to open the door. The handle wouldn't budge. The heavy sound that had preceded the men's departure earlier played through his mind.

Levi tossed the towel aside and punched the wall beside the door repeatedly as he cursed those men—*his business partners*—straight to hell.

Harper laid her hand in between his shoulder blades. "What?"

"They threw the breaker before they left. That was the thunk we heard. The keypad on this room is electronic. Because this is an interior room not designed for occupation, there's no safety release. Code doesn't require one. Once the power went out, the door was effectively force locked."

"We're stuck?" she asked, incredulous.

"Worse than a linen shirt to a fat man's back in the Southern summer heat."

"Better than…" She paused. "I got nothin'." Though she'd clearly aimed for humor, what she delivered was a breathy whisper.

"Your Yoda impersonation counts in your favor. And I wouldn't turn down a badass Han Solo rescue at the moment. Besides," he said, forcing himself to grin over his shoulder and waggle his eyebrows, "I've always had a thing for Princess Leia. What would it take to get you to put on some of those clip-on monster buns and a white sheet?"

She paced the room as she answered. "Work with me to get us out of here alive and the buns are yours. The sheet we'll negotiate."

"Buns, no sheet and I'll get us out of here alive." *I hope.*

"You don't have any negotiating power until my ass is one hundred yards from this burning building." She headed for the shelving. "Where did you put my cell?"

He reached around her and uncovered the phone, handing it over.

She pressed the power button repeatedly, but nothing

happened. "Figures it would be dead, because, you know, nothing can go right for me."

The caustic snap stung and his mind immediately went to their conversation tonight and the climactic kiss. That had been right in so many ways. This wasn't the time to wax nostalgic about it, though. That would come later, as would the guilt. *Later*. "Let me have it. I'll put it in my back pocket and give it back once we're out."

She tossed him the phone and looked up, chewing her bottom lip. "Are the ceilings tiled through the entire club?"

He started pushing the boxes in front of the door again. "No. The club and bar area have plaster ceilings. The offices, backstage areas and locker room all have tile. But if we go up, we're chasing the smoke."

"And if we stay here, we'll be lucky if there's enough left of us to identify by dental records." She hauled a bar stool to the center of the room and hoisted herself up. Maneuvering the ceiling tiles aside, she coughed at the influx of acrid smoke. She collapsed on the stool, fighting to catch her breath.

Levi snatched several cotton napkins and a bottle of sparkling water. Dousing the napkins, he shoved several in his back pockets before handing Harper one. Something in him eased when she began to breathe easier.

He considered the two tiles she'd moved. Now that the crawl space was open, he could hear the threatening rumble of the fire's building momentum. Ventilation ducts ran along the ceiling, suspended by brackets from the roof. Decking for electricians and plumbers ran along the crawl space to keep them from falling through the floor if they ever had to go up. Unfortunately, it was made of plywood—highly *flammable* plywood. There didn't seem to be many—or any—alternatives, though.

Harper stared into the crawl space and froze. The panic on her face had him whipping around. The fire had fully engaged. Flames glowed brilliantly somewhere near the hole in the ceiling, and he knew beyond a shadow of a doubt that their window to get out alive was closing. Rapidly.

"Get up there and park yourself on the makeshift catwalk the maintenance guys use. I'll follow. I've got a handful of wet rags. Keep one over your face the best you can."

"Can you find your way out?" Her chin quivered.

"I'm going to follow the smoke flow. It'll move toward a fresh air source. You're going to crawl. I'll touch you on the right or left to direct you to the external vents. Just follow my touch, okay?" He considered the way her skirt clung to her curves. "Can you crawl in that skirt?"

Without a word, she unzipped it and dropped it to the ground. She wore a pair of black lace boy shorts that hugged her hips and beautifully exposed the creamy swells of her ass.

Later. There would be time for that later.

She didn't meet his gaze as she hopped up on the chair. Covering her mouth with the cloth, she lifted a bare foot for him to help hoist her into the crawl space. One strong shove and she disappeared into the smoke-filled darkness.

Crawling up onto the stool, he pulled himself into the tight space.

The air was saturated with smoke. Staying as low as he could, he nudged Harper in the direction of the nearest exterior wall. She moved quickly, but he noticed the sweat running down the backs of her legs and the way she would falter now again, either coughing or trying to protect the bare skin that scraped along the rough catwalk. And all the while, the temperature continued to climb at an alarming rate.

Harper slowed down.

Through the haze he could see flames licking at everything remotely combustible within their reach. He leaned to the side and realized her shoulders had slumped and her head was hanging forward. A harsh cough racked her body, dislodging one knee so she swayed toward the catwalk's edge.

Dropping his face cloth, he grabbed her hips and re-centered her on the narrow board. "Fifty more feet and we're there, Harper. Don't quit." Smoke filled his lungs. It took only seconds for the blaze to steal the air from his chest. Coughing, he pressed a fresh napkin over his face and forced one on Harper.

Swaying, she took it, her grip weak.

"Move!" he shouted over the fire's now deafening roar. When she hesitated, he slapped her ass.

She lurched forward. Swaying wildly, her progress could only be measured in fits and starts. They were less than a dozen feet from the ventilation grate when she collapsed.

Levi abandoned his face cloth. His lungs burned from the inside as he fought to haul her into his arms. Then it became a matter of clutching her sweat-slickened skin as he walked on his knees across boards beginning to char from the fast-moving fire. The last three feet were brutal. He felt his skin drying up, and he feared he was blistering.

Sirens sounded nearby.

They wouldn't be here in time to save her.

Shifting around to sit, Levi adjusted the unconscious woman in his arms so she sprawled limply across his lap. Then he kicked the grate. Once, twice, three times. It held.

Fury flooded him. He didn't want to go out like this. The men who'd set the building on fire had done so thinking he was inside. They'd gambled his life, and Harper's, for their own safety. No doubt they would make sure he took all the blame if he met his end as the club burned. His friends would never know the truth. His parents would believe him a criminal. And the woman in his arms… He wanted those Princess Leia buns.

Leaning back to gain the most leverage possible, he kicked as hard as he could. The grate popped free. Fire licked at the boards around him. Orange flames cast an eerie flickering glow against the smoke that rushed toward the widened opening.

He scooted to the edge of the ventilation channel. The promise of fresh air was there, just outside the building. Tightening his grip on Harper, Levi dangled his legs over the edge, took as deep a breath as he could and jumped.

11

Harper's throat was still ferociously raw thirty-six hours after the fire. At least the emergency-room doctors had released her the same day she'd gone in via ambulance. She'd spent the majority of her time convincing Daniel to stall and give her a couple more days to wrap this case. Everything she needed to shut Beaux Hommes down was in her files and on her phone. But if Daniel showed up, it meant she'd have to turn Levi in. She wasn't ready for that. Speaking of Levi, he hadn't been so lucky with the hospital staff. While Harper had suffered only minor smoke inhalation, the doctors were concerned Levi had damaged his lungs. The attending physician had insisted on admitting Levi for twenty-four hours of observation. Today he'd left her a voice mail saying he'd been released and wanted to see her.

She hadn't called him back. Not yet, anyway. She had no idea what to say to him. What was the appropriate thing to say to someone who'd saved your life? *Thanks* would never be enough, and abject adoration would make her feel weird, no matter how appropriate it might be. She owed him more than simple gratitude, though. Without him, she'd have died in that building. The truth wasn't lost on her, and no amount of gratitude seemed sufficient.

Then there was the matter of the kiss. She'd wanted to object when he'd moved on her, had wanted him to genuinely *want* her, not act solely out of compassion. But every protest she'd had dissolved the moment he'd cradled her face. That single tender act, so genuine in execution, had leveled her. Years of loneliness had worn her down like a predator with easy prey, and she'd wanted nothing more than for him to slay the unwelcome emotion.

And with a skill born of true compassion and heat betraying an attraction that wouldn't be denied, he'd done just that. He'd coaxed her deeper into his arms until submission to his dominant will was as natural as the sun rising from the eastern horizon.

Then she'd panicked.

Before she could do anything about it, before she could kiss *him* and put herself back in the game, she'd smelled smoke. Rediscovering her passion had instantly taken a backseat to survival. And she still had a case to close—one that had become infinitely more complicated, and much bigger for her career.

For all her heart and mind understood that, she found herself craving the way Levi had made her feel sexy and desirable in that suspended moment, craving his attention, craving his companionship.

The first made sense. She hadn't had sex in more than five years, and Levi was an exceptionally attractive man.

The second was understandable. She hadn't had genuine male interest in a long time, not unless it was shallow and judgmental. And she neither wanted nor needed that particular type of attention from her lovers.

But the third... Over the past week, she'd come to truly like Levi, looked forward to seeing him every day and thrived on the nearly gregarious togetherness she experienced with him. It had happened so quickly, her transition from disinterest to a very personal appreciation for the man he was offstage, in real life.

That third factor alone had driven her to seize the opportunity to put physical space between them while the hospital held him. She'd always maintained she didn't want their relationship to grow personal. It hadn't grown so much as it had mushroomed into something terrifying, something she couldn't quit thinking of even now. When she should be focused on the case.

The first few hours after her release from the hospital, she'd boxed up the files she'd taken from the office before it went up in flames. She'd then rented another car using an alias the IRS had issued for a previous case. Most tedious had been switching hotels, but the Fairmont Olympic was very secure, located in one of the most desirable areas in the city.

Once settled, she'd used the hotel's business center to answer emails, update her boss and ask Daniel to get to Seattle as soon as possible. After the fire, the director had threatened to pull her back to DC. She'd provided a medical release proving her suitable for active duty, but she knew she'd have to prove it with something bigger— closing this case.

And Daniel? He would be here soon enough and had promised to bring her a new gun. She'd feel better once she had it.

The video she'd taken with her cell phone had beaten the odds and survived the fire. She owed Levi for that, too. If it hadn't been for him, she never would have had the video of Kevin retrieving large bags of pills while essentially confessing that the owners owed him huge for his efforts.

The owners.

Levi telling her the truth had been a moment she'd never thought she'd see. Yet it wasn't as satisfying as it should have been. Now that he'd confirmed he was on the books as one of Beaux Hommes's owners, she wasn't sure how to handle him. Because while the phone had picked up the other men's conversation and Kevin's self-narrated activities, it had also recorded her conversation with Levi, all the way through the kiss. The battery had died, the recording ending abruptly, right before she'd broken the intimate connection.

Her fingers went to her lips, tracing the contours. She could still feel the pressure of Levi's lips on her own, their uncompromising demand affording her no quarter to protest his actions. Or had it been affection? Worse, it could have been sympathy, coming on the heels of her asking him if he'd ever given up on his dreams.

Her shoulders hunched defensively despite the fact she was alone. She didn't know how to classify Levi or which mental and emotional box to relegate him to.

Absently sipping her coffee, she tried to focus on the spreadsheets in front of her. Wasted effort at best as the numbers blurred into nonsensical patterns. This was pointless. Her mind had latched on to Levi—his smell, his taste, the feel of him under her hands—and wasn't letting go. She had to admit he was far more interesting, even in retrospect, than the spreadsheets were. And that was a real problem.

Hot coffee splashed down her front when a sharp knock sounded at her door.

No one knew she had registered at this hotel.

Cursing beneath her breath, she plucked her shirt away from her skin. She'd survived the fire without more than scraped knees, but she'd ended up burned due to frazzled nerves.

Go figure.

Scooping up her pepper spray and cuffs, she sidled up to the door, visually double-checking to ensure the deadbolt, chain and door jammer were all engaged. They would prevent someone from opening the door, but they wouldn't do jack to stop bullets.

The way her heart thundered, she had to wonder if her unexpected visitor would hear it. She peered out the peephole, and her heart stalled.

As if conjured by her thoughts, Levi stood in the hallway. His eyes were still red, and his lips were chapped. He leaned a forearm against the door.

"Open up, Harper."

His voice...God save her, but his voice sounded as if someone had taken a rake to his throat. She hesitated. "How'd you find me?"

"Everyone leaves a digital trail. You're well aware of that. Thumb drives register plenty of user data if you know how to mine it. I do." His shoulders sagged. "I'm alone. I'm also busted-ass tired. Just let me in, okay?"

Undoing her safety measures, she opened the door and stepped back.

He took in her pepper spray, cuffs and the door jammer as he entered. "Do me a favor and don't spray me, cuff me or brain me with that iron hammer." Pausing by the bed, he started to pull his shirt off but stopped. "A little help?"

Words totally escaped her. "A little help with *what*?"

The sigh that escaped him sounded almost gravelly. "Help me get in bed. The hospital loaned me the scrubs and flip-flops because my clothes were trashed, but the shirt won't stretch." He shuffled around to face her. She waggled a hand between them and then between him and the bed.

"Bed, Harper. I need sleep." He blinked slowly. "I can't go back to my place any more than you could stay at your first hotel. No doubt the other owners and Kevin have heard we survived. I can't stay with friends because it would just endanger them. You're my only option." Swaying softly, he whispered the last.

He's here because I'm his only option.

An automaton would have moved with more grace than she exhibited as she retrieved a pair of scissors from the desk. "How're your lungs?"

He sank to the edge of the bed. "I'm breathing, aren't I?" When he glanced up, their eyes met. "Since you're holding a sharp, pointy object, I should probably clarify my earlier statement."

She waited.

"I'm glad you're my only option."

"Why's that?" she asked, tone bland as she strove for indifference.

"Truth between us." Levi took her hand. "There's nowhere else I'd rather be."

Totally unprepared for him to drop something like that at her feet, she silently closed the distance between them and grabbed the front of his shirt. She didn't ask for permission.

Instead, she just started cutting.

THE AIR AGAINST Levi's heated skin was an unspoken benediction. As Harper worked, revealing more and more skin, he relaxed. He'd tracked her down using the computer at the nurses' station. That the charge nurse had allowed him to use it at all was proof he hadn't lost his charm entirely. Small reward, that. Having narrowed down the general area he figured Harper had fled to, he'd had a cabbie drop him three blocks from here. He'd searched on foot, hating the paranoia that had ridden him like a two-dollar bet at the Saturday races, forcing him to constantly look over his shoulder, stick to the shadows and generally keep his head down but eyes open.

Then he'd come into the Fairmont, convinced the concierge to let him borrow the computer in the complimentary business lounge and found her. And when she'd opened the door, he'd had the unerring sensation he could finally close his eyes and not worry about whether he'd wake up again. He was with the woman who haunted his every thought, both waking and sleeping. Better yet, she was divesting him of his clothes. Too bad he couldn't enjoy it.

With a click, the air conditioner kicked on, and Harper's scent flowed to him on that initial rush of artificially cooled air. He sighed. Then her hands brushed across his pecs as she folded the scrub top away. The movement was slow, calculated not to put too much pressure on his chest. That wasn't how his cock interpreted it, though. Not even close. Beneath the green cotton pants, the randy bastard swelled with arousal. The hospital hadn't provided him with underwear, so he was gunning commando at the moment. The head of his arousal grew, outlined against the thin fabric.

Harper paused, eyes on the developing bulge in his lap. "If you get this worked up over a pair of generic scissors, I'd hate to see what a red Swingline stapler would do to you."

He grinned, wincing slightly at his chapped lips.

She touched him then, soft as a butterfly's kiss. "Do they hurt?"

"Just a bit."

Leaning forward, she placed a small kiss on the insignificant wound.

"I hurt in a lot of places," he murmured against her lips.

"That's too bad, because you don't look like you're in any condition to…deal with it."

He pulled her close again, pressing their mouths together and sighing when she took control of the kiss.

Her lips roamed over his, tender and almost apologetic. The tip of her tongue traced the undamaged skin of his upper lip, tasting him with soft licks punctuated by rapidly increasing breaths. At her encouragement, he opened to her. She danced her fingertips down the valley between his pecs then lower still, stopping to trace circles around his belly button before sliding to cup his waist. And all the while, she made love to his mouth.

She broke away far too soon.

Looking up, he forced himself to focus on her face and ignore the increasing throb that made his arousal twitch. "Miss me?" he asked gruffly.

"Nope." Reaching forward, she ran her hands over his skin, skimming her way to his shoulders. She was the epitome of gentleness as she helped him out of his shirt. "You've got to be exhausted." A quick glance at his groin. "Well, most of you, anyway."

"I can hardly keep my eyes open and he's down there doing calisthenics."

"Some guys have all the luck." She smiled when she spoke, but the emotional undertone didn't match the teasing words. In fact, it struck him as a bit more reserved than the intimate moment warranted.

"Harper?" He pushed to his feet. Holding his hand out, he held her tentative gaze with his own very direct stare. "Come sit by me since I can't seem to make my mind and body cooperate."

Reservation still decorated her face even though she did move to sit a couple of feet away from him.

He took her hand in his. "You're sending mixed signals, Harp. I definitely don't want to push you too hard or too fast, but I need to know I'm not the only one experiencing this thing happening between us."

Her hand tightened around his. "And what would that thing be?"

Lifting the hand he held to his mouth, he nipped and kissed each of her fingertips until she shifted in her seat. And that's what he'd wanted to see—that he affected her the way she affected him.

He couldn't contain the smile that spread across his face. "Why so skittish?"

"This isn't right, Levi. No matter what…" She hesitated, her gaze skipping from surface to surface as she fought to look anywhere but at him.

Levi reached out and gently captured her chin. "Talk to me."

"Don't you get it? What we want doesn't matter. Not anymore."

His damaged lungs burned deeper, harder and hotter than they had in the fire as he struggled to catch his breath. "Care to explain how you came to that conclusion for both of us?"

She shook her head in apparent disgust and glanced away.

"Uh-uh. The dismissive crap might have worked when we first met, but no more. Explain to me why *this* isn't right." He fought not to raise his voice, to keep it utterly level, when he said, "After all that's happened over the last few days, I think we owe each other honesty at the very least."

Her gaze slid his way, more detached than moments before. "It would have been easier to accept if you'd offered me the truth to start with."

"You're right." His stomach twisted up as if it had been dumped into an automatic bread machine set on knead. And the *real* truth was that he was still withholding a critical piece of information from her: Kevin's daily ledger. He still couldn't bring himself to hand it over.

With the club a pile of ashes, he didn't have to worry about his men. They were all, including him, out of a job. That didn't resolve the issue of his parents, though. Knowing prison was a certainty, he had to wait until he'd moved enough cash to the joint account he held with his dad to ensure his parents would be taken care of while he served his sentence. Then he'd give Harper the ledger and all the work he'd been doing on his own. While he hadn't identified everything Kevin had falsified, he had enough sorted out to be confident he was pointed in the right direction.

"Levi?"

His gaze met the wide gray eyes of the woman whose compassion he'd misclassified as vigilantism. She'd set out to do the right thing from the beginning. All he'd done was put obstacle after obstacle in her path to ensure his freedom while he worked to clean up the most egregious of the criminal activity. He'd wanted to protect the employees from losing their jobs and, even more so, to protect his parents' financial security. But at what point did his self-righteousness become its own bad investment? The answer that had eluded him settled clear and definitive in his mind.

Now.

Levi had taken an honorable woman and baldly lied to her. Then he'd blanketed her in his own prejudices. And he'd wrapped up his one-man show by breaking his personal oath to never use his body as a manipulative tool.

He wanted Harper, but for all the right reasons, wanted to see where this might go if they could get past the investigation and its complications. Only they didn't have much time. How could they have a relationship if he was in jail?

He gripped her hand harder.

Relationship. The word sneaked in and struck him a direct blow to the solar plexus, driving every ounce of air from his lungs in a rush. A coughing fit ensued, saving him from having to explain what had thrust him into a state of near panic.

He'd gone into this thing with Harper practicing intentional deceit. Then he'd upped the ante on his own, deciding to flirt with Harper and keep her mind on anything but the heart of the investigation. And now, for his encore, he realized he'd gone and done the most egregious thing of all.

Levi had fallen for Harper Banks.

12

BEFORE HARPER COULD get Levi to explain what had drained every ounce of color from his pinked skin, he grabbed her and pulled her into his arms with renewed strength. He spoke fervently into her hair, his voice low and emphatic but unintelligible.

"Levi?" she ventured, attempting to lean away from him so she could see his face.

His mouth came down on hers, firm and insistent. There was a sense of desperation in his kiss, something that said he'd had a personal epiphany that had cracked the foundation of who he was or had always thought he'd been.

Caught up in the kiss, she reveled in the strength of his hands as they encouraged her impossibly closer. His mouth dominated her, teeth nipping sensitive skin before his tongue soothed the tiny hurts. He shifted her across his lap and made a sound of approval. Or had that been her?

His rampant erection was caught in the friction of their every move. She rolled her hips and earned a deep groan of appreciation from the man beneath her. The length of his arousal was impressive, scalding her sensitive skin through her cotton shorts.

The kiss escalated rapidly until hands had joined tongue

and teeth. Harper stopped thinking. Everything Levi did felt so good she didn't want him to stop. She could regret it later.

Twisting to better face him, she flattened her palms on his chest and moved so that she had one knee on either side of his thighs. His hands rested at her waist.

She stared down at him and his pupils were blown with lust.

"I need you."

Swallowing hard, she nodded. "Okay."

Apparently that was all the encouragement he required. He shifted them until she was lying on the bed and he was moving up her body with slow but undeniable intention. He paused when their exhales mingled intimately. "Okay," she said again. He slid one hand around the back of her neck and, eyes wide-open, pulled her mouth to his.

Harper refused to second-guess herself. She couldn't fight the feelings she had for Levi any longer. She was through. It was time to take a page from his book and be honest, to acknowledge she wanted this man without apology. It was time to stop being a coward. Anxiety bled out of her body as he wound his large, capable hands around the back of her neck and threaded his fingers through her hair to cup her head and bring her mouth to his.

She gave herself to the kiss, mastered not only by Levi's skill but his gentleness, as well. His lips, firm against hers, were demanding in their presence yet compromising in their pressure. The way he traced his tongue along the seam of her mouth drove her wild. And when she opened to him, when he nipped her bottom lip then soothed the sharp spot with a lazy sweep of his tongue, a soft sound of pleasure escaped her.

He'd snacked on something both sweet and salty recently, the lingering taste of the treat decadent on his tongue and now shared with her.

Her mouth watered.

He swept one broad hand down her neck, over her shoulder and rested it on her ribs, the pad of his thumb caressing the lower swell of her breast, tempting and teasing.

More. She needed more. Arching into his hand, she gasped as he brushed his fingers over the hard bead of her aroused nipple. Her breasts drew impossibly tight, aching for his touch, his lips, the heat of his mouth. The need to touch him, to reciprocate this pleasure, drove her insane.

He ignored her encouragements to hurry, instead rolling her over and continuing to move over her with barely-there whispers of fingertips and, bless him, the mouth she craved.

A strangled choking sound escaped her when he moved away from her breast to trail his fingers down her hip and still lower until he reached the edge of her shorts. He traced a finger around the back of her knee and then up, slipping it under the edge of her shorts and pushing the material up. Not much. Just enough to let him grip her upper thigh hard and, at the same time, grind his pelvis into hers as he delved deeper into her mouth.

She gasped, her hips thrusting forward of their own volition to meet his.

Their tongues tangled. Deep sounds of pleasure rumbled through his chest to echo in hers. She reached for the buttons on her shirt with hands that shook. Desperate to shed it, she wanted to give him access to the sensitive places of her body that had gone so long without a lover's touch. She wanted to allow herself to feel everything, to give him rights to her body, rights she'd granted only to a couple of men in her life. She wanted to touch and be touched, taste and be tasted, give pleasure and be pleasured. All of it. She wanted all of it.

Levi's hands closed over hers as she scrabbled at the

buttons on her shirt. Lifting his upper body away, he broke the kiss. "Slow down, Harper."

The gravelly scrape of his voice and the rapid rise and fall of his chest advertised loud and clear he was struggling to take his own advice.

"I want to touch you," she whispered. Reaching out, she ran her hands over those chiseled abs and the obliques that helped form the cut V on either side of his waist. Her fingers brushed over the smooth skin, tracing the line from his belly button to his waistband.

Muscles tightened and his back bowed up as he sucked in a harsh breath. His eyes never left hers as she learned his body's topography.

A faint smile pulled at her lips. "Not much finesse considering your reputation as headline dancer," she teased.

He grinned absently, the heat in his gaze scalding her. "I don't have a lot of finesse at the moment. We'll try that approach later."

Her throat tightened. Breathing, usually an involuntary reflex, became a conscious effort. She propped herself up on one elbow, resting her hand on his chest. His heartbeat drilled into her palm. "Later?"

The way his eyes darkened made things low in her body spasm. Her fingers curled into his pec hard enough to draw a sharp breath from him.

But then he leaned into her touch, closing the distance between them. His lips brushed hers when he whispered, "Yes, later. *Much* later."

Silently thrilling at the implications that this was more than a moment of madness, that there would be a later for them, the last of her reservations were swept away.

Their mouths fused with a kind of desperation she hadn't anticipated. His body trembled beneath her touch as his hands slipped between them, deftly unbuttoning her shirt.

She worked to get the knot of the drawstring on his waistband undone, yanking at it when she couldn't get the tie to cooperate. Then his hand was there, closing over hers to tear the string out of the pants. The material dipped, allowing his erection partial freedom, and the thick length jutted well above his waistband. Desire drove her to grip him and stroke, to run her thumb over the broad head and smooth the bead of moisture around the cap.

He shuddered under her touch. Raggedly pumping into her fist, his eyes were wild with passion. "Harper."

Her name on his lips, half plea and half promise, pushed her deeper into lust's clutches. She fell willingly.

Levi stood abruptly and reached for Harper's shorts, stripping them off with total economy of motion. He gently touched the tender areas of skin damaged in the fire, his own injuries secondary to hers. "I'm so sorry."

"This isn't about…that." Shaking her head, she sat up, grabbed the tail of her shirt and shrugged out of it.

"Sweet hell," he muttered, his gaze roving over her body with possessive authority. "There are so many things I want to do to and with you that I'm not sure where to start." He reached around to unhook her bra, sliding it down her shoulders. It hit the floor, a hiss of silk over cheap carpet. His broad, capable hands cupped her breasts, thumbs and forefingers manipulating her nipples with expert pressure.

This was only the beginning.

The smell of warm skin drew Harper down. She tugged his pants to rest around his thighs, thrilling at the realization he'd gone commando. His cock bobbed. She glanced up at him and stopped. He was staring down at her with undisguised need, blue eyes wide, pupils blown as he fought to stand still under her touch. She ran a hand around his hip and dug her fingers into his ass.

He jerked forward.

Running her free hand up his thigh, she teased a finger

across the seam of his testicles before grasping the root of his arousal. Her tongue darted out to trace the underside of the corona.

"Baby," he rasped, hips thrusting toward her.

She closed her eyes as she slipped her lips over the broad head and slowly eased her mouth down his thick length. The musky flavor of his body and the salt on his skin were aphrodisiacs of the strongest kind.

His fingers wove through her hair and fisted.

Tightening her grip on his ass, she gently encouraged him to thrust into her mouth. They found a smooth rhythm almost immediately. Eroticism, intimacy, hunger, need— they all moved through her with a carnal brutality. She increased the tempo.

His voice was barely audible when he said, "You've got to stop, baby. I can't hold on."

She hummed around him. But she didn't stop.

Hands fisting tighter, he pulled free of her mouth and hauled her head back. A faint sheen of sweat gilded his skin in the lamplight. "You're amazing, but I don't want our first time to be a solo performance. I want to push you to the brink of insanity and then watch your face as I drive you over the edge and you come apart in my arms. Then I want to follow you."

He hooked his arms under her knees and pushed her across the bed. Stepping out of his pants, he grabbed his wallet and pulled out a short strip of condoms.

The sound of foil ripping made her shiver, and she watched him roll the thin barrier down his thick length.

He dropped to his hands and knees before her on the bed. Soft kisses and sharp nips marked his progress as he prowled up her body. "Anything I need to know?"

She couldn't get her brain to work. "Know?"

He paused, nibbling her hip between words. "Boundaries. Areas or actions that are off-limits."

"Nothing," she breathed. "No boundaries."

With one swift shift he parked his shoulders between her thighs and dragged the flat of his tongue up the crease of her sex. Her hips came off the bed.

Levi wrapped his arms around her thighs and pulled her back down. "Be still."

"Can't," she panted.

"You will," he responded, lips pressed to her intimate flesh.

His mouth worked her sex hard, repeatedly driving her to the brink of release and stopping. The tip of his tongue danced around the knot of nerves she most needed him to touch, but he didn't linger there long enough to satisfy. He teased. He stroked. He suckled. And then withdrew. She shook like an addict going through withdrawal.

It was finally too much. "Finish me, damn you!"

The mattress dipped as he lunged up her body. Slipping an arm under one of her legs, he lifted, blatantly exposing her cleft to him. The head of his cock slid through her folds, seeking.

Harper lifted her hips as much as she could, encouraging him to claim her.

He paused, tearing his eyes away from their joining and dragging them up her body to meet her hooded gaze. "Help me in, baby."

She reached between them, twisting slightly, and then he was there.

With a steady push, he was past the tight entrance, filling her as she'd never been filled before, stretching her to the point she cried out.

He slowed.

No way could she allow him to stop. Not now. Not when her sex was aching for more, to be owned, used, filled and fulfilled. With a sound somewhere between desperation and frustration, she dug her nails into his hip and lifted her pelvis. The move drove him into her core.

He sucked in a breath even as she tightened around him. "Don't be gentle, Levi. Love me hard."

Withdrawing slowly, he gripped her chin and forced her to meet his gaze. "Hell, yes."

The first driving thrust of his hips pushed her up the bed several inches, and Harper had no doubt he'd give her exactly what she'd asked for.

13

THE ABILITY TO think clearly had abandoned Levi even before Harper had swallowed his cock. But from that point forward, everything became a matter of sensation. Her mouth tasted of spearmint toothpaste. The feminine smell of fabric softener on her shirt lingered when he nuzzled her neck. Everywhere he touched, he discovered silky skin. Her sounds of arousal provided wordless encouragements to explore and touch and taste more.

And then there was the sight of her. He'd always been a visual guy, and Harper was an absolute erotic feast he'd never, ever get enough of. The nip of her waist over the swell of her hips, her smoky eyes hazed with desire, the weight of her firm breasts, the hard lines of the tattoos that contrasted sharply with the soft curve of her shoulders, the feminine taper of impossibly long legs, those pink-painted toes—it was as if she'd been designed for him.

Despite the primal need she stoked in him, he'd been totally unprepared when she'd lifted herself off the bed, taking him into her, burying him in her sex all the way to the hilt. His shout ricocheted off the walls. And then her request—"Don't be gentle," she'd said. "Love me hard."

He was powerless to deny her anything. Instinct ruled him, and he was defenseless against its demands.

With her leg still hooked over his arm, he parked his forearm next to her head and slipped his free hand under her body to cup her ass. He pressed up, tilting her hips to receive him as he slowly withdrew. Then he drove forward on a guttural "Hell, yes." Only his arm above her shoulder kept Harper from being shoved across the bed. She gasped, rolling her hips forward to receive him. Her heel dug into the bed in an attempt to gain purchase, to meet his thrusts, but he would have none of it. She was his. She had asked for pleasure. She would take what he had to give.

He grabbed her thigh and pressed her leg open, holding it firmly to the bed as his fingers dug into her firm skin and trembling muscle. Sex had always been about shared pleasure, give and take. Not with Harper. He wanted to own the moment, command her body and demand its uninhibited response. His pleasure meant little. She was his focus. Her hot sheath clenched around him became the center of who he was in that intimate moment.

He wanted to wring her pleasure out, to hear her cry his name, only his name, as she shattered in his arms. He drove into her with purpose, her pleas for more increasing the strength of his thrusts as his hunger for her burned through him, turning his veins to ash.

She bowed off the bed, struggling to lift her hips to his.

He pressed down harder on her thigh and nearly lost it when she groaned and shook under his hand.

"Please, Levi."

Anything. He would give her anything. Shifting the angle of penetration allowed him to rake across the core of her need again and again. Her walls tightened. She gripped his hips and canted her head back, exposing her neck.

He bent forward, covering her body with his, rubbing her clitoris faster, harder.

She exploded beneath him, her pinned hips bucking frantically as she cried out.

Pressure surrounded his shaft, squeezing and milking him as her orgasm crested. He'd thought he'd be able to hold on, to take her higher, but he hadn't counted on the power her release would have over him, hadn't believed it possible that she'd be so uninhibited, had never thought she could command his body and, at the same time, destroy his control. But she had.

The burn of his own orgasm started at the base of his spine. There would be no savoring the escalating sensations. Not this time. The orgasm shot through him with uncontrolled ferocity, tearing a shout from him as he buried his face in Harper's neck and rode out the unmitigated pleasure. He was totally lost to the moment, his body a slave to the release as his hips pumped in spasmodic jerks, his gasps equally tortured.

She rocked against him gently, easing him down. Her fingers traced up and down the hollow of his spine as her body slowly relaxed beneath him. Common courtesy dictated he roll off her. Too bad he couldn't master the necessary motor control to force himself to move. Instead, he lay there and breathed her in.

His hips twitched when she nipped his earlobe, and he smiled into her neck. "I'll return the favor when I can feel my feet."

She rolled her chin away from him, and he lifted his head in time to see her close her eyes. That wasn't going to cut it. Not after what they'd just shared. Levi gripped her chin gently and pulled her face toward his. Soft kisses along her lower lip evolved as she began to respond. He leaned his head back but didn't let go of her face. "What?"

"I…" Swallowing hard, she shrugged one shoulder.

He leaned in to kiss her, working at her mouth until, with a soft sound of acceptance, she let herself fall into the kiss. He stroked her face and neck, letting his hand wander down to cup her breast and thumb her nipple. It hardened quickly beneath his ministrations. Pulling away from her, he softly commanded, "Look at me."

Reluctantly, she did.

"This isn't some crude hit-it-and-quit-it thing between us. You got that?" He bent and suckled her breast, arousal stirring when she raked her fingers through his hair and held him close.

She never answered him, but it didn't matter. Yes, she drove him insane with her argumentative nature and her love affair with rules. Always the rules. And yes, he'd lied to her initially. He could fix that, tell her the truth and set things right. And they might not have a lot of time, but this was *not* over. This was *not* a one-shot thing. Levi hadn't ever experienced anything this powerful before in his life, this raw need for a woman fed by a physical connection he'd never believed possible.

Tomorrow he'd tell her everything. Today? And tonight? He had to figure out how to convince her to give this thing between them a chance, to let her guard down and let him in. No, he wasn't done with her.

Not by anyone's definition.

HARPER INITIALLY BALKED when Levi suggested they fall a little further off the grid.

"Look," he said, shoving his hands through his hair, "if *I* found you, so can they." He began to pace as she continued sorting and reboxing the paperwork she'd been forced to pack willy-nilly when she'd fled the Hilton. "Kevin is an idiot. If I had to wager, I'd place his IQ somewhere between a turkey and a sheep." He glanced at her and shook his head. "I grew up on a farm. Trust me—they're self-destructively stupid. So Kevin's in this mess up to his eyeballs, but he's got to be taking orders from people higher up."

"Makes sense." She put the lid on the last box. "But for all his stupidity, he had the ability to conduct illegal activities in the club without anyone getting suspicious."

He paused in his pacing to scowl at her. "Yes, he did. That makes me think someone on the inside is watching his back."

"Probably more than one person," she replied, absently stacking the boxes to be moved. When Levi didn't answer, she looked up.

He was staring at her, jaw tight and Adam's apple bobbing. "I don't want to believe that the men I put myself on the line for, the very men I'm probably going to go to jail for, helped Kevin pull this shit off."

Harper's belly lurched hard enough she fought the urge to heave. She'd been trying not to accept what it would mean for Levi when she wrapped this case—or what it would mean for her in the long run. "I'm sorry."

Waving her off, he began pacing again. "You're probably right. I just don't want to accept it. No one wants to accept that their family is corrupt." The last was issued softly.

Shifting to glance at him, her eyes narrowed. "What are you implying?"

He shoved his hands in the pockets of the hotel bathrobe. "Kevin had to know you were coming, Harper. He was in the office that morning and left less than an hour before you arrived. Beaux Hommes isn't the only operation that's dirty."

"You're saying someone from the IRS tipped him? The only people who knew I was coming were the director and my partner. Oh, and my dad, but he had no idea where I was going—only that I'd be away for a few days." She crawled into the nest of covers on the bed they'd essentially destroyed. "Daniel wouldn't tell anyone. But the director would have informed the local IRS office that I'd be here in the event I had to call in help." Cold crept along her arms and legs to settle at the tips of her fingers and toes. "Someone from the IRS local office has been covering for the club."

"Seems most logical." He glanced at her briefly before his gaze skittered away and focused on some innocuous building outside. "But if this person warned the others, why didn't he notify me?"

Rising, she went to his side and slipped a hand around his waist. "You were set up as the fail-safe."

He gave her a quizzical look but said nothing.

"A fail-safe is someone the leaders of a criminal ring bring in because they see potential in him. They groom him to start assuming responsibility, rarely disclosing the full range of illegal activities until the fail-safe is so far in he can't get out." She hesitated, unsure how much more to say.

Levi noticed, waving his hand in a drop-the-other-shoe motion.

She rubbed her upper lip, wishing there was an easier way to break this to him. No such luck. "But if things go south, the fail-safe is the scapegoat and he gets tied up in the mess while the senior members get out of harm's way."

Death was no stiller than the man in the hotel robe. He watched her, his mouth opening and closing several times before he finally croaked out the inevitable statement of acceptance. "I was set up."

She didn't say anything. There was no need. They'd both put the pieces together, but as the victim, he wanted a different explanation. Anything would do so long as he had an out for having been played. But nothing she could say, no condolences she might offer, would change the truth.

"They were willing to kill me to protect their enterprise."

Oh, this sucked. "Yes."

"They set the building on fire knowing I was in there."

"Probably." No, she wouldn't hedge the truth. "Yes. I believe they did."

His hands shook, tightening the belt at his waist. "And if I'd come out when they called me?"

"Levi, don't do this."

"I want to hear you say it," he said in that damaged voice.

"It would only be speculation on my part."

He didn't waver, didn't move.

"They would have killed you, Levi. Is that what you want to hear? That they would have shot you or drugged you to the point of incoherence and left you unconscious to burn to death? Or maybe they would have simply hog-tied you and left you to burn with the rest of the evidence." Nearly panting, she couldn't stop the swell of panic that threatened to drag her under. "Is that what you want to hear, Levi? That these men you called partners and friends used you, manipulated you and were fully prepared to hang you out to dry?" An unexpected tear rolled down her cheek. "I've *been there*, Levi. I *know* what it's like. It's the worst feeling in the world. But at least you weren't in love with the person who did this to you."

He turned in jerky half steps and went to her. "Tell me."

So she did. "After my dad's shop went under, I was angry and hurting and…stupid. A guy I knew through the shop, Marcus, was starting his own business with a friend and begged me to join them. He was charming and smooth and…he paid attention to me. I thought he loved me. My dad worried that Marcus was too good to be true, but I accused him of just being jealous of Marcus for succeeding where my dad had failed. To be honest, I think that was part of Marcus's attraction—I fell for the dream as much as for the man."

She stopped, and he put a hand on her arm, urging her to continue.

"He kept promising that he would make me a partner. But I was so beautiful and sexy, he argued, why shouldn't I be the face and the body of the brand? I was so smart, why didn't I come up with a few more lucrative ideas first? I fell for it all—until the IRS knocked down the door and arrested me."

"Shit," Levi breathed.

"So the day I was exonerated, I decided to stop chasing empty dreams. I could help others who were being played and used—with the law. I joined the IRS."

"And stopped living."

"I stopped being *stupid*. I stopped being *gullible* and falling for the lies of charming men. I stopped being *hurt*—" Her voice broke on a sob.

He pulled her into his arms and held her as the tears fell. She burrowed into his warmth and strength, sure it would be a long time before she emerged.

14

Loading the last box into the truck he'd borrowed from Cass, his best friend's girlfriend, Levi adjusted the sweatpants Harper had charged to the room from the hotel's gift shop. They were a little tight but better than nothing. The T-shirt, though? It was obscenely tight. He'd actually split a seam at his shoulder as he'd moved boxes around. He had a whole new level of sympathy for the Hulk.

He'd convinced Harper to take up Cass's offer to let them crash at her apartment. Cass was trying to sell the place, but she'd contacted her real estate agent and asked him to take it off the market for two weeks. Since the place was staged and in a highly secure building, it would serve Levi's purpose well.

But he was worried about being in such close quarters with Harper. Knowing the owners of the club, men he'd trusted, had been willing to kill him to preserve their interests had scarred him. His faith in humanity shaken, he'd found himself cautious with Harper. He was afraid to reveal just how wrecked this experience had left him. Yet, at the same time, it had given him an intimate look into what she must have gone through when her ex had done the same thing to her. Granted, Marcus hadn't put her in a life or death situation, but by Harper's own admission, she'd loved the guy.

And after her admission, he understood just how much pain he could inflict on her—because he was still lying to her. But maybe if he could explain, she'd understand why he'd had to keep things from her. Maybe despite the lies and her job—and the fact that he'd likely face some serious time as the State's guest—they might be able to find something together. Something long-term. Even…

Yeah, right. You just got played by the owners of Beaux Hommes. Don't add to the mess by playing yourself and picturing something, craving something, that can never be.

Levi slammed the truck's tailgate harder than necessary.

Harper rounded the passenger side of the truck and tossed her suitcase in the back, keeping her messenger bag with her. "Ready to go?"

"Yeah."

She hopped into the cab after he opened the door for her. "Before we pull out of here, I want to remind you to watch for anything that seems out of place. Doesn't have to be overt, just off."

Her comment cut into his thoughts, pulling him back to reality. "Why?" He covertly glanced around, feeling idiotic. Shrugging the feeling off, he shut her door, crawled behind the wheel and took off. He didn't speak until they were merging onto the interstate. "You don't really think they're going to come after us in broad daylight do you?"

"Accidents happen, Levi. Cars blow tires and roll, semis swerve and cause multicar pileups. People fall down the stairs in their apartment buildings and break their necks." She huffed out a breath. "I know I sound paranoid, but these are legitimate concerns."

He switched lanes. "I'm not stupid. Keeping a low profile is why we ended up borrowing Cass's new truck versus something more familiar. It's why we're moving into her place temporarily. It's why we can't go out much until this is resolved."

Until I can make sure my parents are taken care of and then turn myself in.

"I didn't say you were stupid," she said levelly. "Just reminding you to be cautious."

"Sure." He appreciated that she hadn't arrested him the minute he got to the hotel, though it showed a level of trust in him that he was only going to betray. He tightened his grip on the steering wheel. He'd brought the ledger with him. It had been risky to go back to his apartment and retrieve it, but it had been the only option left to him if he was going to prove to her his intent to be totally honest at all costs.

The place had been ransacked. Drawers had been empty, furniture destroyed, pillows shredded, his mattress sliced open. They hadn't thought to check the frozen pizza box, though. Retrieving the ledger, he'd forgone clothes so he wouldn't have to make up another lie to Harper about why he suddenly had clothes. Hell, he'd even borrowed one of Eric's beat-up briefcases, intent on leaving it in the truck until he could sneak it inside.

He had no doubt whatsoever that she'd be pissed when she learned what he'd done. But he'd done it for *her*. Learning what his business partners were capable of had stripped him clean of any illusions he'd held about life being just and fair. If they'd been willing to kill him, someone they each knew and had been partners with, they wouldn't hesitate at all to take an IRS agent out, female or not. Levi could only hope they believed the ledger had gone up in flames with the building and that he intended to cut and run. Another reason to fall off the grid. Because otherwise? The odds of them leaving him and Harper alone were nil.

Mind wandering, he found himself stuck on a particular subject. "Harper?"

"Mmm-hmm?"

"Did you know the field office had a mole? Is that why you haven't called them in for help?" He ignored the way she stiffened in her seat and finished the thought. "Or is there some other reason you haven't mentioned to me?" He figured her past probably drove her to succeed, but what did she have to prove? Surely her coworkers respected her for her commitment. She'd been given this case to work solo, so clearly they had faith in her. So why did she insist on carrying so much weight when she could have shared the burden with her peers?

Silence hung between them, an invisible, impenetrable barrier of differing priorities. She went so long without answering that he relaxed his hold on the steering wheel. He'd almost decided to let the subject go when she answered in a voice so low he had to lean toward her to hear her.

"I had no idea there was a mole in Seattle, but the reasons I didn't call for help are very personal. I explained what went down with me and Marcus. And while I like you, I won't let all the skeletons in my closet fill up your personal dance card. They don't dance for anyone's entertainment but mine."

A sharp pain shot through his chest, and all he wanted was to gather her in his arms and comfort her again. Things were very different today than they'd been last night. So he said, "Entertainment, huh? I think I'd rather go see the new Avengers movie."

Her choked laugh was better than the seriousness with which she'd answered. She surprised him when she said, "I heard it was really good."

"Maybe we can catch it when this is all sorted out." The spontaneous offer to take her out on a date—*a date*—stunned him in its ridiculousness, and, from the widening of her eyes, the feeling was mutual.

"I live in Washington, DC. Once I wrap this case, I'll be on to my next assignment."

It bothered him that those skeletons she'd mentioned—Marcus and love and loss and betrayal—would still haunt her. She'd started over with nothing, had had no one to lean on and no one she could trust. He understood how lonely that must have been, and must still be, but it hadn't truly registered until that moment when understanding and firsthand experience settled into the seat of his consciousness with a kind of raw acuity that scraped at his common sense and grated across his emotions.

Part of him wanted nothing more than to forget he'd made any effort to know even the smallest personal thing about her. The other part, though…well, that part was the problem. He'd never been drawn to a woman like this, had never wanted to take it upon himself to show her there was life after heartache.

Sure, he'd been a rebound guy more than once. But that had always been between the sheets, and that made the whole thing somehow different. Harper wasn't rebounding. From what Levi had seen, she'd effectively walled herself off and stopped taking any chances in life. She walked and talked, ate and breathed. But she didn't live.

It was asinine to think he could be the knight to her broken heart. Not when he'd be the one to crush what was left of the pieces into dust.

HARPER WAS EXHAUSTED, her clothes were wrinkled, she was hungry and now she smelled like Chinese food thanks to Levi's yen to grab a couple bags of takeout on their way to the mystery apartment. She wasn't grumbling about the food, though. Besides, it wouldn't have mattered. He wouldn't have heard her protests over the prehistoric roars her stomach emitted every few seconds.

And no matter how tired she was, her workday wasn't

over. Far from it. She figured if she could push through until about 4:00 a.m., she'd grab three hours of sleep, a shower and breakfast before tackling the new day by eight. With the peace and quiet the apartment offered, she should be able to figure out a way to close this case without sacrificing Levi.

Her gaze traveled to Levi, darting away as he moved and offered her his profile.

Maybe. Maybe *I'll be able to get a lot done.*

Continuing to deny what he did to her, at least in the privacy of her thoughts, was pointless. When she combined his brain with the brawn in that gorgeous package and added in his ability to make her knees weak with one kiss…yeah. Totally pointless. Still…

She chanced a second glance his way, watching as he loaded boxes onto a luggage cart he'd borrowed from a bay near the elevator. The muscles in his shoulders worked, bunching and releasing, his biceps flexing. The long muscles of his back were pronounced enough to forge a valley that followed his spine. And that was a seriously. Fine. Ass.

How long had it been since she'd looked at a man and allowed herself to experience this unrestrained rush of attraction? If she were being honest, Marcus was the last one who'd affected her that way. No. He'd been the *only* one to affect her that way. No one else had ever been able to fuel such a volatile sexual hunger in her.

Until now.

Irritation sang along her nerve pathways, firing beneath her skin with aggravated little pops of awareness every time she appreciated something new about Levi, from the slight wave in his thick, shoulder-length hair to the way the hollow at the base of his throat begged to be kissed and the way he'd offered her exactly the kind of comfort she needed. Her shaky inhale sounded loud in her ears. Given the faint sheen reflecting off his skin, she would bet she'd taste the subtle, salty tang of sweat if she traced her tongue through that hollow. Her teeth sank into her bottom lip.

What is wrong *with me?* He was a suspect, and right now the only one she had.

Blinking quickly, she leaned against the truck, giving him her back while she regained her composure. She was tired. That's all this was—a perfectly normal adrenaline crash after nearly being burned alive and experiencing the best sex of her life. All compounded by exhaustion after a long flight and a series of very long days in a different time zone.

"Sell it like you survive on the commission, sister," she muttered, moving to the rear of the truck to help unload boxes. No matter how she tried to decorate her feelings, the truth was the truth—she was falling for Levi. It didn't matter that he was part of the investigation. It didn't matter that he threatened her career. And above all, it didn't matter that he'd lied to her. But it did matter that they had no future. So the sooner she accepted that yes, he made her fire on all cylinders, the sooner she'd be able to control herself and direct the outcome between them. No harm, no foul. He was a man; she was a woman. Even if it didn't typically—ever—involve her, chemistry happened. She'd suck it up and move on.

Right. Tough talk over.

She slammed the final box down on the cart and moved aside as Levi rounded the rear of the truck, the last box from the backseat in his hands. His brow furrowed as he looked at the stacked boxes. "Did you unload these?"

"It was only a few boxes."

He set the box he carried on top of the precariously balanced stack. "They were the heavy ones."

A single brow winged up of its own volition as she considered him. "You're not seriously going to reduce me to hovering because I'm wearing a skirt and heels, are you?

Because I sure didn't put you in panty hose when you asked me for styling cream for your hair earlier."

He laughed and then put his shoulder into the cart to get it moving. They rode the elevator to the eleventh floor where she followed him down the posh hall to a nondescript door. He dug out the keys and ushered her inside, pulling the cart with him.

She felt his eyes on her before he spoke. "Hungry?"

"Mmm-hmm."

"Thumb wrestle you for the chicken egg roll."

Her laughter was sudden, a spontaneous thing she hadn't been expecting in the slightest. "Thumb wrestle me?"

He shrugged. "Sure. They only had one left, and I want it."

Narrowing her gaze, she leaned against the foyer wall with calculated insolence. "Did they give you sweet-and-sour sauce?"

"Hot mustard, too."

"You're on, but be prepared, Levi. After midnight, only a fool comes between me and my egg roll."

"I'm nobody's fool." At her mock threat, he smiled.

Harper's heart stuttered. How had they gone from her shoving her way into his office a week ago to her essentially hiding out with him? Even doing a quick replay of their time spent together, she couldn't make sense of it. One thing was clear, though. Whatever fracture he'd caused in her defenses had been subtle but undeniable, and when he'd kissed her? When he'd leaned into her and cupped her face and stroked the seam of her lips with his tongue? When he'd settled his hips against hers, his arousal an undeniable presence against her belly, and branded her with his heat? When he'd taken her this afternoon, showing her just how good it could be between them? When he'd held her as she cried? It was then that the very foundation of her defenses had been compromised.

And while she was no emotional engineer, the structural damage seemed so significant she wondered when what seemed like a house of cards would collapse.

15

SOMEWHERE BETWEEN SLEEPING and waking, Harper realized she was burning up. Sweat dampened her back, so she rolled forward and pitched the covers off. A heavy arm tightened around her waist, hauling her into the heat source. *A body. A hot, hard,* very *morning-male body.*

She smiled. Last night—*all night*—had been amazing. Levi hadn't let her get near the files. He'd raided Cass's wine fridge and together they'd knocked off two bottles of red. It was the first time in years she could remember truly relaxing in someone's company. That the someone she'd enjoyed so much happened to be Levi Walsh, stripper, financial prodigy, loving son and criminal in the eyes of her employer still surprised her. He'd been awesome, from making her laugh to rubbing her feet to loving her body and making her let go of her reservations and inhibitions.

She stiffened as snapshots of the evening flipped through her mind, an absolutely erotic mental photo cube. She sucked in a breath, remembering when Levi had… *No. I didn't actually* do *that. Did I?* As sore as she was, she had to believe she had.

Part of her fought not to blush. Not the majority of her, though. No, not even close. The majority of her was of the opinion that Levi should receive some kind of sexy-time creativity medal. Oh, and one for sexual stamina. And probably something to acknowledge his exceptionally capable follow-through on dirty talk. She couldn't remember a single thing he'd suggested that he hadn't delivered on before she fell asleep. That particular award was definitely well deserved. Hell, they all were.

But no matter how great the night had been, he was still a confirmed accomplice in her case.

The contented smile that had been playing around her mouth faded. The sun peeked around the edges of the Roman shades, a stark reminder that regular life went on. What they'd experienced had been remarkable; she wouldn't take that away from either of them. But that didn't change the fact it had to end. She'd fully expected the chemistry between them would be insane if let off the chain, and she'd been right. What she hadn't expected was her emotional reaction. For the briefest moment, she'd felt connected to someone again. She hadn't been lonely. She'd woken in a lover's arms, solid and sure. The reminder of just how good it could be left a void in her chest that made it hard to breathe. She hurt, and she'd sworn she'd never let another man hurt her ever again.

Rationally, she knew it was in no way Levi's fault that she was emotionally defective. That blame lay at another man's feet, part of a past she felt she'd never be able to outrun, no matter how hard she tried. Punishing Levi for her own flaws wasn't fair. Expecting him to navigate dark waters with violent undertows when she herself could barely keep her head above the surface was totally unrealistic.

A sob locked in her throat, and she pressed the heels of her hands against the unexpected burn in her eyes. Unable to lock everything down, a shuddering breath escaped.

Levi's arm tightened around her at the same time his

lips pressed into the hollow at the top of her spine. "Good morning, darling."

"Hey." The stranglehold of her emotions exaggerated the morning rasp in her voice.

He relaxed his hold on her, trailing his hand up over her shoulder and down her ribs before coming to rest possessively on her hip. Long fingers absently stroked the crease between her thigh and sex. "You sleep well?"

"Yeah." Her mouth was so dry she felt as though she should be spitting sand with every word.

Without warning, Levi swung a leg over her, his body following. He wrapped his arms around her waist and rolled onto his back, taking her with him and placing her solidly on top of his arousal. He gripped her hips when she shifted to accommodate the pressure of his hard cock. He groaned and his hips pumped upward, short and sharp.

The movement tipped her forward and forced her to park her hands on his pecs. That left her staring down into shrewd, albeit aroused, blue eyes. When she tried to sit up, he bent his knees, feet flat on the bed, effectively trapping her where she was. Heat burned across her cheeks. The need to cover her body, to protect herself from the type of vulnerability wrought by such intimate exposure, frustrated her. She'd never been bothered by nudity. In truth, she wasn't bothered so much by it now. What left her so fundamentally naked was the understanding in Levi's eyes. His gaze roamed over her, lingering on her breasts before he took one nipple into his mouth. His eyes rolled up to meet hers.

Again, she shifted, this time with more authority.

His breath rushed out as he pulled her tighter to his groin as he thrust upward. Thumbs stroking her hips, he let himself relax against the bed. "You want to talk before or after?"

She blinked rapidly. "Talk? After what?"

"Morning sex." His palms slid over her lower belly to cover her pelvis, his thumbs slipping through the folds of her sex with only a whisper of a caress.

Sucking in her breath, she laid her hands over his to still them. "There can't be any morning sex, Levi."

"Then we'll talk first." He was so damned agreeable, but he didn't move his hands. Or his thumbs.

How was she supposed to have an intelligent conversation when his thumbs, one on either side, were pressed lightly against her clitoris? Every breath, whether his or hers, moved his thumbs without fail. It was a constant, uninterrupted stimulation, the kind that built with slow persistence until her body became single-minded in its interests.

She rested her hands on his wrists, gasping when he began to rock against her, his caresses growing bolder, the pressure intensifying. "Stop," she breathed.

And damn if he didn't. Fluid motion one second, still as stone the next. His nostrils flared. "Harper," he said in a soft but uncompromising tone. "I told you the first time this wasn't the kind of thing where I—*we*—blew off some steam between the sheets and then disappeared at dawn." He settled his hands on her hips, grip light but firm. "You agreed."

Hooking one hand over her opposite shoulder, she nodded.

He tilted his head to the side as he considered her. "Then what's the problem, baby?"

Her breath hitched. "Don't."

"Don't what?" he asked, brows winging down in obvious confusion.

"Call me baby." She forced herself to relax her grip on his wrist. "I'm not holding you to anything you said after the fire, so you don't have to pull the affectionate morning-after thing with me. It's okay."

"It's okay, huh?" His tone was calm, almost disconnected.

Awareness tapped up her spine in a series of dance maneuvers that rattled her. "Yeah."

"What if I don't agree?"

"Huh?"

"What if I don't agree that it's cool to call it an experience and walk away?" The muscles at the back of his jaw worked. "What then, Harper?"

"Don't complicate this, Levi." She moved off him, and this time he let her go. "We enjoyed ourselves and I…" She ran a hand around the back of her neck and squeezed. It had been on the tip of her tongue to tell him she didn't regret it. And she didn't. But that wasn't the right sentiment for the moment, particularly because he seemed so on edge. Switching tactics, she gathered her clothes from the floor and dressed. "We have a lot to accomplish today. I'd like to remain focused on the case and not get sidetracked by any unnecessary personal issues."

"Unnecessary…" He rolled out of bed and grabbed his sweats, jamming his legs into them with near violence before rounding on her. His mouth opened and closed, but no sound came out. Dropping a shoulder against the bathroom door frame, he rested one ankle over the other and crossed his arms. His lips were compressed, a thin, harsh fault line of temper.

Despite the anger rolling off him, Harper couldn't help but stare. The drawstring of his sweats was loose, the waistband dipping to reveal the base of his cock. He was semiaroused and thick enough to create an impressive bulge under the cotton. She silently cursed herself and looked away. Encouraging him wasn't fair.

"Don't try to shut me out, Harper. You'll just piss me off."

Shock had her facing him without concern for the desire that still burned between them. "Don't piss you off?"

"You heard me," he drawled.

"So, what—this is about your temper now?"

"You know damn good and well what this is about." He shoved off the door and took a step toward her, pausing when she backed up. "You're busy blaming history or your job or my job or geography—anything you can come up with that will let you put this experience in a box in your mind so you can go on living like the zombie you've been since you joined the IRS."

"A few days working together that culminated in one night in bed with me doesn't mean you've changed me. You don't know me, Levi." She thumped her fist over her heart, her voice ragged. "Not my background. Not my history. Not my experiences. Not my limits. Not my fears. Not *me*." She spun away from him and started for the bedroom door.

"Then let's not focus on what I don't know and take a hard look at what I *do*." Two giant strides forward and he reached around her to slam the door shut just before she got there. Eliminating the distance between them, he planted one hand on either side of her shoulders and caged her in his arms.

"Wow me," she whispered, despising the note of undiluted hope that colored the challenge.

"Oh, I can wow you. You just have to be brave enough to not only hear it, but to freaking *listen*." The taunt blatantly dared her to run, said he expected it.

So she stood her ground and prayed it wouldn't fall out from under her.

LEVI'S INNER VOICE was so loud it drowned out the heartbeat thundering in his ears as it shouted obscenities and threatened self-inflicted misery if he screwed this up. She'd attempted to shut down on him, and he'd panicked. Not his proudest moment, but as the panic morphed to anger, he'd found himself challenging her to hear him out. It had been the only thing he could come up with—prick her pride. Now? He had to find the right words to make her hear him because this was, in all likelihood, a one-shot deal.

What he got instead was a rush of word vomit. "What do I know about Harper Banks? She's complicated, layered and so much more vulnerable than she initially appears. Rules are important to her because they give her structure. Sticking to the rules in her professional life helped her find success, but she can't seem to find hard-and-fast rules to live by in her private life, so she chooses not to have a private life, or to live at all. It's safer that way. She doesn't adhere to the 'no risk, no reward' theory since taking risks doesn't come with rules but rather best guesses, and guesses won't cut it. Not for the woman who insists life is strictly black-and-white, the woman who, until this week, shunned every shade of gray she encountered. How am I doing so far, Harper?"

He leaned over her shoulder, settling his cheek to her ear as he tried to ignore the rapid rise and fall of her shoulders.

He continued, "She's loyal, even blinded by it at times. But once she's in your corner? She's there. There's this huge capacity for compassion in her that she really hates to expose, considering it a weakness when, in fact, it's one of her greatest strengths. Trust has burned her, so she doesn't offer it easily."

A fine tremor shook her, and he wanted nothing more than to stop what felt like a verbal assault, wrap her in his arms and provide her with a guaranteed safe harbor. Not that she'd accept it, but that didn't stop him from wanting to offer it. Instead, he closed the distance between her back and his torso, determined to finish this so if—or when— she ran, they'd both know he saw her for who she was. If she didn't change now and start living, she'd forever be the coward she feared she was.

He drew a breath and the smell of her warm skin made him close his eyes and dip his chin lower so they were cheek to cheek, his morning stubble to her softness.

"Stop it," she breathed.

"No." He pressed on. "The woman is made up of a thousand sensual components and is a goddess in bed, for all that true intimacy terrifies her. She fears unguarded moments. Still, the sounds she makes when she gives in to her arousal are the sexiest sounds to come from a woman's mouth. Ever." Pressing his body closer to hers, he feathered his fingers down her arm, brushed over her fingertips and paused at the hem of her skirt. "She wears the most erotic lingerie under the most boring clothes, and she thinks no one has any idea—" he pressed a soft kiss behind her ear "—but I do." He gripped her skirt and worked it up, one-handed, until her bare ass was revealed.

The conversation wasn't supposed to have taken them back here. His intent had been to talk to her, to make her not only hear him but to listen, to recognize that what they'd had meant something, even temporarily.

But he was burning for her, his skin drawn too tight. His fear of losing her took over, hijacking his body and using it as a communication tool.

Sinking to his knees, he nipped the curve of one cheek, his cock rousing at the very feminine sound that escaped her. When he spoke, he kept his lips pressed softly against the creamy flesh. "She has a handful of erogenous areas that she makes her lover work to find. It's totally worth the effort." He gripped her hips and rose to plant small kisses along the sway of her lower back, listening for any indication she wanted him to stop.

None came.

He let his fingers wander forward. A breath he hadn't

realized he was holding escaped when she arched back and spread her legs, welcoming his touch. Gently working through the folds of her sex, he slid first one and then two fingers inside her, slowly and rhythmically pumping in and out of her.

"In bed seems to be the one place she doesn't get hung up on rules. She's the most creative, generous lover a man could hope for, passionate in her responses and determined to give as well as she gets. But above all?"

He pulled free of her and stood. Shoving his sweats down, he bent his knees and, fisting his cock, fed himself slowly into her receptive wet heat. Her moan of pleasure was gratifying, but when she widened her stance even farther, presented herself fully and reached back to grab his hip, he had to fight to control his body's reaction. He took her free hand and stretched it over her head, palm against the wall. Lacing his fingers through hers, he began to move, rolling his hips, nearly pulling free of her before burying himself deep with every thrust.

"Above all, there might be a hundred more things I know about her, but there are thousands left to learn." He increased the pace, the erotic slap of skin against skin coupled with her soft sounds of encouragement creating a sexual soundtrack that drove him higher. "For the record, *baby*, I intend to commit myself to learning every… single…one."

Her hand gripped his hard. The way she rocked her hips to meet his every thrust forced him to adjust his stance and hold her hip tighter. He wanted to slow down, to make this last, but she only rode his shaft harder when he tried.

Without warning, she increased the tempo even more, her hips thrusting harder, faster, her muscles tightening around him. There was a heartbeat of surreal silence, and then she cried out.

He pulled her back against his chest, thrusts shallow as

she mindlessly rode out her orgasm. She shook violently in his arms and he was almost ashamed when he lost himself in the moment, his own release claiming him. He was a slave to his climax. Unable to stop what they'd begun, he tried to simply bury himself inside her and let the storm pass so he could hold her. All he wanted was to hold her.

A single sob escaped her.

In the midst of pleasure the likes of which he'd never known, her broken sound raked at his soul. Their lovemaking had crossed an invisible line. This wasn't sex, wasn't a sharing of two bodies with a common goal. This was a convergence of two people who hadn't realized they were looking for each other.

Until now.

16

HARPER SHUT THE shower off. Steam twisted in lazy wisps up and over the shower curtain. She shivered. Grabbing a towel and drying off made sense, but it meant she'd have to pull the curtain back. Levi was on the other side. Waiting.

Faced with the impending conversation with him, being cold wasn't so bad.

He'd refused to leave her alone in the bathroom and had only let her shower without him after a short argument. She'd needed some space. Her mind was an absolute maelstrom of emotions. There wasn't room for an overbearing lover hovering over her while she tried to understand what had happened between them.

Lover.

She shivered again, though it had nothing to do with being cold. Quite the opposite.

Lover.

Levi is my lover.

Hands down, he was the best lover she'd ever had, but that had little to no bearing on what they'd shared. Or maybe it did. Maybe it was part and parcel of the bigger picture. Maybe she'd been emotionally unplugged for so long that she could no longer recognize the correlation between someone accessing a riptide of sexual desire she hadn't known she possessed and at the same time finding herself rendered emotionally bare. No, not bare. What he'd done was far more complicated than leaving her bared to him.

He stripped me raw.

And now he wanted to talk about it.

"You coming out or do I need to come in after you?" The question was soft. The promise buried in it? Not so much. His shadow moved, growing more defined the closer he got to the semitransparent curtain. Metal rings rattled as he pulled the flimsy barrier aside. A low-slung towel clung to his hips, dipping dangerously low beneath his navel. "Come in after you it is."

Apparently she hadn't answered fast enough.

She fought the urge to cover her breasts; it wasn't as if he hadn't already seen it all. His gaze was intense as it roved over her in a proprietary manner, leaving her feeling vulnerable and insecure. Both were unfamiliar and decidedly unwelcome. Whereas she'd normally strike out at anything that made her uncomfortable, that wasn't really an option anymore. Levi wouldn't take her crap and would give back the very same she dished out. That meant there would be no running. Not anymore. And not from him.

That last concession struck her hard enough to make her dizzy. She reached for him at the same time he reached for her, and their hands met halfway. Ironic in the most nonhumorous of ways that she would meet him halfway on anything. Since Marcus, it had been her way or the highway in almost everything. Reminding herself again that Levi wasn't Marcus, she let him help her out of the deep tub and accepted the towel he offered. "Thank you."

"You're welcome."

She dried off before wrapping herself in the towel. Then she faced him. Nerves, like butterflies the size of small birds, made her stomach flutter. Meeting his steady stare proved harder than she'd expected. Her gaze drifted away, her thoughts struggling to coalesce into something she could articulate without sounding foolish or desperate.

Strong, capable hands cupped her neck. Subtle pressure turned her face toward him, and he dipped low enough to snare her focus as he traced one thumb along her jaw. "We're going to talk, but I'm not going to force you."

"Apparently all you have to do is drop your towel," she muttered.

His lips twitched. One hand dropped away from her neck and before she knew it, his towel had fallen away to pool at his feet.

"Cute." What should have been a sharp comment totally failed, emerging as a croak.

"Not exactly the response I was after, but we can start there."

The teasing undertone pulled her chin up as effectively as if he'd moved it by hand. She arched one brow. "You don't want to be cute?"

He leaned in and feathered a light kiss over her lips. "To you? I'd prefer to be irresistible."

Her heart stuttered before taking up a jackhammer rhythm against her sternum. A caustic comeback would have created at least a little distance between them. But for the first time in a very long time, she didn't want to disconnect. And she definitely didn't want to risk saying something that might hurt him. Difficult as it was, she went with the most basic, most terrifying thing she had in her arsenal of possible responses. The truth. "You're definitely that, Levi."

A low-level hum emanated from his chest. He pulled her in close, wrapping his arms around her and resting his cheek against her damp hair. "Lucky me."

Being held by him felt right in every way. Unsure of

herself but determined to prove she could handle intimacy with him, she carefully wrapped her arms around his waist and held on.

Levi drew her closer, eliminating any space between them.

They stood there for several minutes, neither speaking. The silence ate at Harper. She was only delaying the inevitable, and she knew it.

But how were they supposed to talk about this? How was she supposed to make polite conversation about the most basic, fundamental side of herself?

As if he'd heard her, Levi loosened his hold on her and leaned back, dropping his chin to his chest so he could see her.

"Clothes first then talk, okay?" He nodded, and she allowed herself a quick grin. "Seems everything I have is trashed after your exuberant 'Disrobe Harper' plan of attack last night."

"I have no regrets." One corner of his generous mouth lifted. "But I bet Cass would be willing to pick up something that would work. She could even drop it off. No one will think twice about her being here. A T-shirt and sweats okay?"

"Sounds awesome."

"Until then, it's got to be the towel. Or..." He took her hand and pulled her into the bedroom, grabbing his T-shirt and offering it to her. "You could wear my shirt. Just until she, uh, gets here."

She accepted the shirt and slipped it on before dropping the towel, conscious of the way his eyes warmed.

He came to her, running his hands up and down her arms before kissing her swiftly. "I like seeing you in my shirt."

Her thoughts scattered like spilled mercury. "Why?"

Leaning around her, he picked up his sweats and stepped into them—all without answering.

She waited.

He dropped his hands to his hips but didn't look up when he spoke. "Don't run."

The words were so low she almost thought she'd misunderstood him. Then he glanced up and she knew better. A single, unguarded moment abjectly exposed his worry when their eyes met. Surprise whipped through her. Two words. Paired with that look, they conveyed so much.

"I won't."

His Adam's apple bobbed violently as he swallowed. He tipped his chin toward the living room. "Would you mind sitting on the sofa? I think it would be best to get out of the bedroom for this conversation."

Her heart plummeted, shooting past her stomach as the latter catapulted up the back of her throat.

Some part of her reaction must have translated to her face because Levi grabbed her hand. "No! No," he said more softly. "If we stay in here, I'm not going to be able to keep my hands off you. And if things get a little or even—" he dragged his free hand down his face to pinch his chin "—a lot uncomfortable, we need to talk it out. Without a doubt, we manage incredibly well in bed, but there has to be more to conflict resolution in a relationship than screwing each other senseless."

Relationship? Harper couldn't find her balance. "Sitting down would probably be a good thing."

Still holding her hand, he led her into the living room, moving some paperwork aside so they could face each other on the sofa. He settled her first then sat close enough their knees touched.

He started to say something, but she cut him off. "One thing."

"Okay."

"Promise me, Levi."

Taking her hand, he twined their fingers together, his focus on that uncomplicated union. "If it's within my power to make and keep the promise, then yes. I'll promise you whatever you want."

"Don't lie to me," she rasped, embarrassed at the desperation in her voice. "Promise me you'll always tell me the truth no matter how hard it is. Too many people have lied to me, whether to spare my feelings or so they had better leverage to screw me over. I can't…" She blinked rapidly. "You claim this is more than sex, more than…" She exhaled in a sharp puff. "You've used the word *relationship*. It can't go that far for me. Not unless you promise to keep the truth between us no matter how hard it is. Promise me you won't lie to me anymore."

Eyes widening slightly, his grip on her hand tightened as he nodded.

"Tell me, Levi. Say it." There was no compromise in her demand, but she couldn't help it. Her gaze strayed to their hands and stayed there.

She'd been lied to far too often and hurt far too badly by the people who had claimed to love her most. If she was going to believe what Levi had said to her last night and again this morning while he'd been buried in her, loving her body like no one ever had, she needed this from him. It would be better to know now if he couldn't give her this one thing. Laying her other hand over their joined fingers, she stroked his wrist. "The truth. Please."

"I promise not to lie to you, Harper," he whispered, the words gruff. "Truth, always. Even if it hurts."

She closed her eyes and nodded. Fine muscles in her arms and legs trembled for a moment before she could get them under control.

Truth, he'd said. *Even if it hurts.*

The truth, *her* truth, was that she was falling for Levi

and had been since that door hit him in the head. He'd looked up at her with wide-eyed shock, but she'd been the one struck dumb.

Gripping his hand even harder, Harper took a deep breath and gazed up into somber blue eyes. And right then, in that singular moment, Harper made the hardest choice she'd ever made.

She put hope in front of history, and she chose to dream.

LEVI LET GO of Harper in order to pull her into his arms and bury his face in her neck. Trying to ignore how right it felt to hold her, how right it felt for her hands to stroke his back, was pointless. His chest nearly seized, the sensation sharp and brutally painful.

What the hell was he thinking? The promise he'd just made wouldn't have been a big deal at all…if he hadn't still been lying to her. Man, he was criminally stupid. What he should have done was seize that particular moment to come clean, to tell her he'd had possession of Kevin's ledger all along. That he'd intended to work with her every day and spend each night amending the screwed-up journal so it matched what she'd found. *That* was why he'd brought her the thumb drive every morning and taken it home every night. It had nothing to do with loyalty.

He could have produced the ledger then. He could have shared what he'd learned. That would have opened the door—hell, the *avenue* for him to plead for her forgiveness and guarantee her she'd get nothing but the truth from him ever again.

Instead? He'd lied *again*, landing himself deeper in the bog of bullshit he'd created with the first lie and filled to overflowing with every lie thereafter. Currently hip-deep and sinking fast, he was losing any hope of redemption as he drowned right where he stood.

He'd never been deceptive or manipulative or secretive.

The fear that had driven him to be these things had been for those around him, those who mattered most. He'd acted to preserve their well-being.

Guilt, heavy as a baseball made of uranium, dropped low and heavy in his belly.

Proud moment right there, man. Lying to yourself.

Apparently there was no end to the lengths he'd go to absolve himself of guilt. Levi knew with absolute surety that it hadn't been only friends and family he'd wanted to protect. Both then and now, there existed the highly probable chance that he could lose everything and face a prison sentence. Wouldn't *that* be awesome when the news made its way to his hometown of twelve hundred people.

The gossip would destroy his parents. They'd always been so proud of him. He'd been the first in the family to go to college, and then he'd found financial success in the city. Every time he went home, they treated him like some kind of hero. The thought of losing their admiration, and particularly his old man's respect, had struck him dumb and blind. So when put on the spot, he'd lied to protect himself.

In the end, no matter how he spun it, the entire mess came down to one very fundamental truth—the fault was on him. He had to hold himself accountable. Not Kevin, or the other owners or even the IRS. *Himself.* But first he had to know that Harper would be okay.

Her cell vibrated, startling them both. She reached behind her to snag it off the table, but he caught her wrist and shook his head. "Ignore it. There are a few things I want to talk about before we dig into this mess."

"Okay." Shifting to face him, she squared her shoulders.

Despite the razor-sharp tension, he couldn't help but smile at her. "You don't have to face off with me like we're MMA cage fighters waiting for the bell."

Her face darkened, the corners of her mouth turning

down in consternation. "Yeah? Well, in my experience, these talks usually leave both parties bloodied and beaten, and there's rarely a clear winner. Humor me."

Levi reached out, grasped Harper by the back of the neck and pulled her forward. Off balance, she fell into his lap. He twisted, pulling her under him and pinning her to the sofa, his hips settling between her legs.

He moved without thinking, canting his head so his mouth fit over hers. Deft feminine fingers wove through his hair and pulled him closer, demanded more from him and gave just as much in return. She spread her thighs wider beneath him, and she tilted her hips to cradle him firmly against her sex. No one would blame him for ignoring the phone when it rang again. Particularly when he realized she still wasn't wearing underwear.

Sliding a hand under her, he gripped her ass. "Did I mention how much I like you in my shirt and nothing else?" he asked, voice like gravel.

She arched into his touch. "This isn't the kind of Q and A I'd geared myself up for, but carry on."

Emotional vertigo forced him to plant both forearms beside Harper's head for stability. Arousal that had built so quickly crashed, a critical support piece he didn't recognize he'd needed pulled out from under him like a bad Jenga move. He pushed off of her and stood to button his jeans. "I'm sorry."

"Sorry? Why?" Harper sat up slowly. "What just happened?"

He raked his fingers through his hair, shoving the length away from his face. "I want to talk to you, make sure we're on the same page before this goes any farther."

She tucked her knees to her chest and pulled the shirt over them and down to her ankles. "So talk." Defensiveness emanated from her like a radioactive glow.

This was his best chance to drag himself out of the shit

bog, even if it left him needing a bleach bath to get rid of the stink. No way was he going to hurt the woman he'd spent his entire adult life looking for due to his own hubris.

Comprehension dawned rather slowly, but when it hit? It leveled him more effectively than Godzilla taking on downtown Tokyo.

The pervasive discontent that had dogged him the last couple of years finally made sense. He'd been lonely and waiting for the right woman to come along. Granted, he hadn't waited passively. Hardly. Looking back, though, it all made so much sense—the unsettled feeling, the desire for more than a singularly physical experience and the deep-seated craving for what both Eric and Justin had found. Watching those two with their women had been so hard.

"Levi?" Harper stood, crossing her arms under her breasts.

Rising from the sofa in slow motion, he shook his head. "Gimme a minute."

He had to get his head screwed on straight. Jumping into something long-term with Harper had seemed impossible before. But what was the alternative?

The thought of not seeing her or hearing her voice ever again, of truly being without her finally brought passion and purpose together for him. He knew what he wanted and, for the first time in life, what he needed. More important, he could differentiate between the two, assign both want and need independent values that, when added together, equaled the whole of who he was.

He was the man who was head over heels for Harper Banks.

17

THE SKEPTICISM AND WARINESS in Harper's gaze tore at Levi, but the knowledge of what he was about to do to her gutted him.

He took a step toward her, stopping when she backed away in equal measure. "Harper."

"Why are you looking at me like that?" Curious terror. That was the only way to describe the tone of her voice.

"I want you to understand how hard this is for me. It was never supposed to get this far."

Her eyes flared and she froze. "What?"

Right. Probably could have made better word choices there, dumb ass. "This is coming out wrong." His hands trembled as he shoved them through his hair.

"Just say it." Her whisper broke on the last word.

"I care about you," he started.

She wrapped her arms around her middle. "But?"

"But nothing," he snapped.

"Right. Because every conversation that starts with 'I care about you' always ends well, Levi. *Always.*" Color crept up her neck and stained her cheeks. She threw her hands up and turned in a tight circle, her gray eyes flashing a banner announcement that her temper was brewing.

"You know what? You're not doing this to me. I won't let you. Screw you, Levi Walsh."

She started for the bedroom.

He intercepted her, grabbing her upper arms and holding on tight, unsure whether it was for her benefit or his. "Listen to me."

"Go to hell," she snarled, struggling against his hold.

The only choice she left him was to spin her and wrap his arms tight around her torso, pinning her arms to her sides. "Stop it, Harper. Don't make me take you to the ground."

Her struggling stopped. "Say what you want to say and then let me go, Levi, or I swear to God I'll make you regret the day you met me."

Dipping his chin, he rested his cheek against her hair. "Never." Her total lack of response scared him. "I care about you, Harper. Enough that it disturbs me. I can't get you out of my head. It's constant. Day and night you're there, always on my mind. This is all new to me, and while I'm willing to go down this road and essentially throw myself on the merciless sword of your history, I have to clear something up. I made you a promise, and I'm going to keep it. You deserve no less."

She didn't respond, but the weight of her silence weighed Levi down, a leaden yoke of purpose.

He took a deep breath. "I promised you the truth." Then he let Harper go, trying not to react when she scrambled away only to round on him.

"What have you done?" The question was delivered in complete monotone, as if she was too busy reeling in her emotions as fast as she could to put any effort into inflection.

They wordlessly stared at each other as the chasm of distrust widened. He could feel it happening. Running a hand up and down the valley between his pecs, he blew out a hard breath. "Harper, I—"

Her phone buzzed for the third time.

Levi blew out a vile curse. "Leave it."

As if he hadn't spoken, she stepped around him and snatched up the cell. Swiping the screen to answer, her eyes never left him. "Banks."

He paused and laced his hands behind his head, rocking back and forth, impatience simmering. The sooner she got off the phone, the sooner he could tell her the entire truth. Then they could work together to map out how they'd clear the slate and start over. Admitting the magnitude of his lies would be the hardest part. Really, though, it was the only logical place to start. She'd listen to him. She had to. He'd be willing to beg if he had—

Her violent curse stopped his mental strategizing. "What?"

Whirling away, she stalked toward the kitchen. Spine ramrod straight, her movements were efficient bordering on militaristic. Her voice was low and urgent, but he couldn't pick up what she was saying.

So he followed her.

She'd stopped to lean on the island, free hand fisted on the countertop. Her head hung between shoulders almost brittle with strain. "They have to back off. I need to talk to him before they start in on him." A pause. "I understand they made the capture, sir, but the IRS has both interest and authority in this case, as well. If we'd made the capture, you can bet your ass they'd be demanding their due. Interdepartmental compromise is a game of quid pro quo. They should keep that in mind."

Levi watched her shoulders tighten even more as her legs locked and she slowly rose.

"Kevin Metcalf isn't acting alone. There are…four owners. Two of the four plus Kevin were the ones to lock me and…my stuff in the club prior to burning it down. The men referenced a third owner, indicating he's actively involved.

"Metcalf was in the club to retrieve illegal prescription medications. I have it on video, sir. The official books are clean, so Metcalf must have some other personal record." Her fingers drummed against her thigh as she listened to someone Levi could only assume was her boss. "If the FBI finds his personal ledger and tags it as evidence, it's going to effectively shut down my investigation until either they free it up or we navigate the bureaucratic nonsense the Washington political scene thrives on. Either way, it could take months. Maybe longer." She paused again to listen, this time nodding. "I'm willing to bet I can get Metcalf to disclose where his personal records are."

Sweat blossomed all over Levi's body, and his gut cramped so hard he thought he might be sick. *The ledger. Lie number one. Or had it been two?* God help him, he couldn't keep it all straight anymore. The sequence didn't really mean jack, though, because Kevin would confess where the ledger was—he'd given it to Levi the same day he'd disappeared to set Levi up as the scapegoat.

Oh, shit.

"If that ledger contains the information I believe it does and if I can get my hands on it, I can close this case." A slow, feral grin spread over her face. "I'll be there within the hour. Thank you, sir."

She thumbed her phone off and twirled it in her hand. "Metcalf's been caught."

"How?" Levi's throat had tightened so much he had to force the question through.

"Border patrol picked him up trying to cross into Canada. He probably would have made it if his trunk hadn't been packed with semiautomatic rifles and large-caliber handguns. That got him hauled out of the vehicle and was more than sufficient grounds for a search without a warrant. That's when the officers found the six giant totes of prescription drugs. Apparently Kevin forgot to have 'his' prescriptions labeled before trying to leave the country."

She tsked. "I'm thinking Kevin realized he was in over his head after the fire. He panicked and bolted, taking the drugs as his relocation fund." She raked her fingers through her hair and sucked in a deep breath. "Whatever you were going to say will have to wait. I need to get to the federal building before the FBI if I have any hope of questioning Kevin before they do."

Heart thrashing around in his chest, Levi fought to control his respirations. "Why does it matter who questions him first?"

"He hasn't been officially arrested. Until then, I can advise him he's a person of interest and tell him I'd like to ask him some questions without being required to read him his rights. Chances are good he'll be caught off guard since he won't be expecting me. If he's smart, he'll lawyer up eventually. I want to get as much from him as I can before he does." She tilted her head, watching him carefully. "What?"

"Nothing. Just…listening to you." *Seriously? Another lie? Man, what is* wrong *with you?* If he had any hope of getting out of this with Harper's understanding and forgiveness, let alone the chance to see what they could build between them, he had one option. "I'll take you to the federal building."

"No. Forget it. You aren't part of this anymore. Just get me back to my car and I'll—"

"I have Kevin's ledger."

FOR SEVERAL SECONDS, Harper could only stare at Levi. The words registered as having been spoken. She'd even assigned them individual definitions and parts of speech. But collective value? She couldn't. Her mind had gone completely, utterly and inexplicably blank. His mouth began to move, but an intense buzzing white noise drowned out whatever he said. She shook her head.

He took a step toward her, reaching for her hand.

"Don't," she bit out, whipping her hands behind her and out of his reach. "Don't you *dare*." Chest heaving, she considered him. "How could you sit there on the sofa and tell me you wouldn't lie to me anymore when you were *still* lying to me? I mean, you get that one lie doesn't cancel the effect of another, right?"

Lies. I trusted him and all of it, every damn word out of his mouth, was a lie.

Levi dropped his hands to his sides. "Let me explain."

She laughed, the sound perversely happy, and shook her head again. "I don't think so. You had your chance. More than one, actually."

He leaned his butt against the kitchen island and crossed his arms over his chest. "You know why I kept that ledger, why I had to try to get a handle on things. Those men, *my* men, would have been out of jobs. My parents—"

"I've heard this particular song, including the chorus, and watched the corresponding dance. Save it for counsel." She whipped around and started down the short hall, calling back to him with admirable calm, "All the times we were alone together, all the opportunities you had when you could have owned up to it, you chose not to. That's on you, *darling*. No need to use your people as your crutch anymore. Besides, it all ended up the same, anyway, didn't it?"

"How?" he asked, close on her heels.

She laughed again, but the humor was obviously dark. "Your men are out of work, the club is *definitely* shut down long-term and you're going to do time." Stopping in the bedroom doorway, she refused to face him when she said,

"I feel more sympathy for your parents than anyone else. They're going to have their assets seized all over again because of your choices."

"You leave my parents out of this," he all but snarled.

"You're the one who dragged them into this mess, Walsh. That was all you." She finally glanced back. "I'm just doing my job."

She shoved off the door frame and stalked into the bedroom, decidedly ignoring Levi as she fought to reclaim her composure. The vicious ache in her chest wasn't unfamiliar, but she hadn't been prepared for it. That it surprised her was insult to injury. She didn't remember the pain being quite so debilitating when Marcus had betrayed her.

Marcus.

If there was anything that could make this worse, conjuring his ghost did. She'd spent so much time convincing herself that Levi wasn't Marcus, but Levi was just as deceitful with his statements of loyalty, empty promises and passionate lovemaking. All lies. Particularly the sex. It had just been sex with a particularly talented lover, and she'd let him convince her it was so much more. No doubt he thought her a gullible fool. Cold realization washed over her. She *was* a gullible fool and probably always had been.

With her few belongings in hand, she fought to master her equilibrium as she swung wide of Levi and headed for the living room. Order of business: swallow her pride, get dressed, box up the files, get to the federal building, question Kevin Metcalf…and arrest Levi Walsh.

She stumbled.

Hard hands closed over her arms. "Easy."

This time she heard him, heard that fabulous voice that had whispered to her so suggestively in the dark, felt the strength of the hands that had loved her body so intimately, and she nearly broke. Twisting with as much violence as she possessed, she broke his hold and changed her trajectory, lunging for the bathroom. "Don't touch me again. Ever." Chest heaving, she paused outside the powder room. "Give me the ledger."

"I'll get it while you're getting dressed. I give you my—"

"What? Your word?" She couldn't stop the huff of air that escaped. "I'd rather deal in hard facts, because your word isn't worth shit."

Shutting the door, she forced her brain to focus on the list of tasks she'd run through moments before. This time, however, she omitted the last item. It was so foolish of her, but she couldn't think about arresting him right now. If she hadn't looked over her shoulder as she'd shut the bedroom door, if she hadn't made eye contact with him to force him to see the resolve in her hard stare, she never would have seen the untempered emotion that filled his eyes. She would have missed the way his hands had fisted and his body had leaned toward her. But she had seen it, and she'd recognized it for what it was.

Regret.

18

FOR LEVI, THE BLAND, oatmeal-colored room—walls, ceiling, floor, door—was like being trapped in sensory deprivation hell. The only break in the color scheme was his reflection in what he assumed was a two-way mirror and the dull finish of the metal table and chairs. There was no clock to mark the passage of time. He could have been in here thirty minutes or three hours. Whatever. It had been a veritable lifetime since Harper had deposited him in the room, taking everything but his phone and leaving without a word.

What was left of his pride proved difficult to swallow as he dug out his cell and scrolled down to Eric's number. He hesitated for a moment. *It should never have come to this.* Words he'd now said twice today would haunt him forever. He tapped the screen to initiate the call.

The phone rang twice before the man answered. "What's up, Romeo?"

Knowing it was pointless, Levi still turned from the mirror and lowered his voice. "I need you to make that call to your attorney."

"What happened?" Eric's tension and concern translated fluidly over the line as papers shuffled and a digital Rolodex clicked in the background.

"Can't talk at the moment, but the sooner you make that call, the better." Levi paused, trying to decide how much to say. Screw it. He was essentially in custody. There probably wasn't much he could say to make things worse for him, but he might spare Eric and Justin. "You guys take care of yourselves."

"Crap. Where are you?" When Levi didn't immediately answer, Eric blew out a hard breath. "I have to tell my guy where to find you."

"Federal building, downtown." He closed his eyes. "I'm in an interrogation room, two-way mirror and video camera. No nipple clamps hooked to car batteries, though, so it's cool. Just have the attorney get here as soon as possible."

Eric snorted. "You realize you just ensured a hot nurse is going to show up with an anal probe and feather tickler."

His effort at humor was obviously strained, but Levi appreciated it. Throat unexpectedly thick with emotion, he replied, "Not interested unless the nurse is…" He didn't want to say her name, didn't want to let anyone on the other side of that mirror know exactly what she meant to him.

"Oh, man." The echo of impact said Eric had hit something. "Tell me you didn't fall in love with the IRS agent."

"Do *not* go there," Levi snapped. He didn't care if he was being watched. No one was going to disrespect Harper. And no one was going to make him feel guilty for loving her. "It wasn't a choice for me any more than it was for you."

"Ease up. It's just not the best situation."

"Like it ever is?" Levi's chin fell to his chest. "Look, I appreciate you making the call. I'll obviously be here whenever he's able to make it. And Eric?"

"Yeah?"

"Thanks." Before the other man could respond, Levi rushed on, quiet but determined. "I've envied you and Cass from the beginning. Take care of her."

"Levi—"

He disconnected the call and turned his cell off. There was no one else he intended to talk to, and he didn't want anyone calling him. Eric would pass the word on to Justin. He'd made sure his parents' funds were safe. That meant Levi had done all he could do. The knowledge that it wasn't nearly enough made him sick.

Swiveling back to the table, he laid his head on his arms and did the only thing available to him.

He waited.

HARPER LEANED AGAINST the wall outside Kevin Metcalf's holding room. For the past two hours, she'd used both fear and persuasion to get him to talk. Turned out the guy was a chatterbox full of interesting information, and he'd offered up names like sacrifices to the gods of justice in the apparent hope he'd be spared.

He was an idiot.

"Banks."

As usual, her name sounded sharp and hard-edged when her boss snapped it out. She shoved off the wall and faced him. "Sir."

"That little quid pro quo bit you harped on earlier?" He jerked a thumb to a nearby closed door marked Conference Room C. "Congratulations. It's happening in here, and you're our keynote speaker."

Great. "I should get my report written up while Metcalf's information is still fresh." It was an excuse. What she wanted was to get the hell out of here.

He cocked one half of his bushy brown unibrow. "The interview was recorded. The meeting won't be. Which one do you think you can come back to?"

Understanding she'd be railroaded one way or the other, she walked into the conference room without answering him and went straight to the front of the room.

All but one of the dozen or so agents, all men who wore badges identifying them as either FBI or IRS or ATF, did little more than look her way as she stepped up to the small podium. The exception was Daniel. His mouth tightened when he spotted her and he started to stand. She shook her head, relatively certain he saw through the shallow layers of her self-defense to the gaping wound in her chest where her heart had been.

Her boss moved to her side and addressed the room. "Agent Banks is going to give you a rundown on what the suspect in custody disclosed during his initial interview."

"Should've been an FBI matter, but whatever," a blond guy muttered.

Daniel leaned in and slapped the back of his head. "Shut up. Metcalf was more likely to talk to her than you, so admit it was the right move."

Much as she appreciated Daniel standing up for her, she ignored both men. She had so little left to give after last night and this morning. If she could get through this quickly, she could get the hell out of there.

Squaring her shoulders brought flashbacks of Levi teasing her on the sofa only hours ago, and her knees nearly gave way. Nothing but stubbornness kept her standing, and only the tattered scraps of what pride she had left helped her to speak. "At roughly oh nine hundred, I began my interview with Kevin Metcalf, male suspect in the IRS's fraud investigation of the male revue club Beaux Hommes. Miranda rights were not read as the suspect has not been charged at this point. I disclosed to the individual that he is, indeed, a suspect. He proceeded without coercion or undue influence."

And so it went. She laid out the facts as she knew them.

Kevin Metcalf was both the middleman and the operation's accountant. He'd run the drugs from one club owner's medical practice to the club, separated and bagged them and then delivered them to addresses that were texted to him. Terms were cash on delivery. Texts always came from different numbers and the locations were never the same. Some of the drugs were kept at the club for customer purchase. All a buyer had to do was go to the bar and ask one particular bartender for a private menu. The bartender then hooked the customer up with the dealer who posed as club security, the transaction was completed out of sight and the customer returned to the show.

After a few days of cash collections, Kevin would funnel money through the club as paychecks for terminated employees or to people whose IDs had been lifted. There were several dancers who had false IDs to match the names and, for a small percentage of the check value, would cash the checks and return the funds to Kevin. There were also exaggerated costs for purchase of goods from the partner who owned an alcohol distribution company. Ridiculously inflated rent for the club, the parking lot and the office complex all went to the third partner through various corporate fronts he'd set up.

A dirty IRS agent had contacted Kevin the same day Harper had arrived. For a pretty price, the agent had warned Kevin that the club was going to be investigated, going so far as to share suspected charges. Kevin had called three of the four partners and warned them. They'd directed him to get rid of the ledger and fall off the grid. Self-preservation had driven him to gather what he could and try to get out of the country.

One of the FBI agents lifted his pen and interrupted. "Did he identify the IRS agent? And what about the fourth partner? Did you get his name?"

"Yes. To both questions." She stared down at the podium. Nervous energy made her pick up a generic pen and start twisting the cap around and around.

"Great. Care to share?" the agent snarled.

The pen fell from her fingers but she made no move to pick it up. Gripping the flat of the podium, she forced herself to meet his arrogant gaze. "The IRS agent is Samantha Browning."

Her boss immediately stepped outside, probably ordering someone to bring Browning in.

The questioning agent leaned back in his seat and crossed his arms over his chest. "Halfway there, Banks. Any reason you're not throwing the fourth owner to the lions?"

"The fourth owner is a club employee. A dancer. His name is Levi Walsh."

"Where is he now?" Daniel asked.

"Interrogation six."

"How'd he get there?" a different agent, this one tagged as FBI, asked.

Sweat prickled along the nape of her neck. "I brought him in."

"You must have been aware from the ownership records of his name. If he didn't run days ago when Metcalf did, why didn't you bring Mr. Walsh in before now?" the same agent pressed.

She hated the FBI, the whole agency, from the part-time janitor all the way to the director.

The agent-from-hell stared at her, waiting.

She'd hoped she'd be able to keep Levi—and their personal relationship—out of it. When Kevin had been picked up, she hadn't needed the recording she'd made at the club.

But had she just been protecting herself? This case had been all about proving she was strong and capable and *the best*. And instead she was just proving to be a coward.

Levi had lied to her both about being the new partner

as well as about having the ledger. Yet he'd also helped her. Right before he seduced her.

But in spite of all of that, he'd forced her during the course of one emotionally volatile conversation to recognize that he *saw* her.

So for the first time in her life, Harper had no idea what to do. How could she come clean and still keep Levi safe? She kept hearing her dad's voice telling her to take the opportunity to do the right thing. But she wasn't sure which thing qualified as right.

Her boss's whiplash voice cracked through the air. "Answer the question, Banks. Why didn't you bring Mr. Walsh in for questioning days ago?"

So answer she did. "I had no evidence he was guilty of any crime, and he was assisting in the investigation."

The agent's grin was malicious. "Oh, I bet he assisted your *investigation.*"

"Let me guess," she drawled, leaning on the podium. "You're a nine-to-five guy, aren't you? Some of us aren't tie-wearing, clock-punching desk jockeys, sweetheart. We work the job and we close the case, even if it means bending the rules."

"So you admit you broke the rules?" the FBI agent from hell asked, a smirk on his face.

Her eyes locked on Daniel's. "Metcalf's account corroborates Walsh's official statement that he had no idea what was going on. He's come in voluntarily and has offered to assist, filling in any blanks he can identify in operating practices or personnel records. At this point, there isn't sufficient evidence with which to charge him." She paused. "But yes, I broke the rules. I'll be tendering my resignation immediately."

Ignoring the resultant chatter, she left the room.

_19_

HARPER HEADED TOWARD the elevators, intent on getting the hell out of Seattle. The local office could wrap things up in cooperation with the FBI and ATF. She didn't need to be here for that. Keeping her pace measured and not breaking into a wild sprint took the last of the control she possessed. She kept her thoughts trained on making it downstairs, catching a cab and going straight to the airport. Her stuff could be donated to charity. Nothing she'd brought was irreplaceable.

Her steps faltered as she passed interrogation six. Was Levi still in there?

She forced herself to pick up her pace, but once she started accelerating she couldn't stop. Every step grew longer until she was jogging.

A strong hand closed over her biceps and spun her around.

Heart in her throat, she stumbled as she pulled away.

"In here. Now." Daniel opened a file room door and dragged her with him, his hold on her tight enough to make it clear he wasn't letting go. He pushed against the pneumatics on the door, forcing it closed with a labored hiss. Then he rounded on her. "Out with it."

"I—I don't know what you're talking about," she sputtered.

His brow creased as his eyes softened. "Such a beautiful liar."

She jerked back.

"What happened between you and Walsh, Harper?"

"Nothing," she whispered.

"You've spent a week with him, a single week, yet I just watched you, *you*, confess that you'd broken the rules to a roomful of federal agents." He tugged at one earlobe. "They might not understand what that means for you, but I do. So I'm going to ask you again. What happened?"

She closed her eyes. "Nothing I won't survive."

"Sweetheart, you're stubborn enough to survive all but a point-blank shot to the heart."

Her breath caught, turning her smooth answer rougher than a cheese grater. "I intend to survive that as well."

Muttering a vile oath, he wrapped her in his arms.

She sagged in his embrace, burying her face against his chest. Hard as she fought against it, the first tear slipped over the dam of her lower lashes and began to trail down her cheek, a tributary for the next tear to follow. And follow it did.

His lips rested on the crown of her head, his hot breath feathering through her hair. "If you don't tell me what happened, I'm going to go in there and arrest him."

Tears fell faster. "You don't have anything to charge him with."

"Given the circumstances, I can hold him on suspicion, temporarily seize his assets and generally make his life a living hell. Seems like fair play given the state you're in." He let her go and stepped back, his dark eyes bitterly cold. "In fact, I think that's exactly what I'll do."

She grabbed his hand. "Don't do this, Daniel."

"Then talk to me, Harper, because no one gets close to

you unless you let them, and he had to get damn close to reduce you to this."

She physically flinched. "Ouch."

He hissed through his teeth. "I want to dismantle the guy, one bone at a time."

"Metcalf gave him the ledger the day I showed up. Walsh intentionally withheld it, going so far as to tell me he hadn't seen it." She swallowed around the lump in her throat. "He lied to me." The truth drew fresh blood and Harper wondered if she really would survive this.

Daniel reached for her again, drawing her so close she could feel his heartbeat. His voice rumbled beneath her ear. "I'm going to kill him. Slowly."

Her answer was caught between a sob and undisguised gratitude. "You can't."

"I beg to differ. I passed the FBI's Methods of Murder and Mayhem class with honors. I'm quite capable. And for you? Anything." He hooked a finger under her chin and lifted. His gaze narrowed dangerously before flaring in disbelief, his face going slack. "Tell me you didn't fall in love with him."

"I didn't," she whispered. "I'm not."

"You don't even realize it, do you?" He hugged her so tight she could hardly breathe. "That lucky bastard."

"I don't love him, Daniel," she insisted, voice undeniably raw. "You know I'm not programmed that way."

He leaned back a fraction, his stare drilling into hers. "So if I wanted to kiss you right now, you'd be fine with it."

Her throat worked. "I'm not in the mood to be kissed, but thanks for the offer."

He leaned toward her, closing the distance between them until their lips nearly touched.

There was no stopping the wave of emotion that rolled over her, dragging her under without mercy. "Please. Don't."

Cupping her face, he laid a fierce kiss against her lips and spoke against them. "That's what I thought."

And that was the exact moment she stopped lying to herself. The truth proved as painful as its reputation, giving her no quarter.

Daniel reached for her.

"Don't," she said, voice breaking. "Just…don't. I have to go."

Yanking the door open, she started down the hall. She grabbed her cell and dialed the only number she could remember.

Her dad answered on the second ring. "What's up, turkey butt?"

A strangled sob broke free at the sound of his voice. "I need to come home, Dad."

"What happened? You okay?" he demanded.

"I can't…" She swiped at the tears raining down her cheeks. "I just need to come home."

"Your room's waitin'. How soon will you be here?" he asked quietly.

"Today."

"Call me with your flight details and I'll be there to pick you up. And Harp?"

"Yeah?"

"If you want to talk about it…" She heard him shuffling and then he sighed into the phone. "I'm here for you, baby."

"Thanks," she managed to squeeze out before disconnecting without a goodbye.

By the time she hit the stairwell, she'd given up all semblance of a controlled retreat, her heels sounding like pistol shots as she ran. But try as she might to escape, the truth dogged her every step. And while she loved her dad, this wasn't something she could share. Not with him.

Because in an impossible twist of fate, Harper had fallen in love with Levi.

LIFETIMES LATER, WHEN the door finally opened, Levi looked up sharply. He'd expected a lawyer. He'd hoped for Harper. What he got instead was one incredibly pissed-off IRS agent.

"Not one word," the man snapped. "Get up."

Levi kept his eyes on the agent and slowly stood.

"Come with me." He pulled the door open and gestured Levi out of the room.

"Where?"

"Shut. Up."

Levi cautiously started out, glancing back at the two-way mirror.

The agent grabbed his arm and hauled him forward, letting him go when they were chest to chest. "Don't look at them. I'm the one you should be worried about."

Levi's hackles rose. "Any particular reason why?" The urge to take the agent's bait and make this physical was a major temptation.

"If you have to ask, you're not as smart as everyone seems to think you are." The man started down the hall and didn't glance back when he barked out an order to Levi to keep up.

Staying a few steps behind, Levi followed the federal douche down the hall into a cramped file room. He slowed, then stopped in the doorway. "I assume there's a reason you want me to follow you into a windowless, unmonitored room."

The stranger leaned against a file cabinet and glared from hooded eyes. He tipped his chin toward the door. "Shut it."

Levi stepped the rest of the way into the room and let the door close. The latch clicked heavily, and all he could think was that it sounded ominously like a prison gate bolting him in.

The room wasn't large enough to brawl, so chances were

good that wasn't why the agent had brought him here. Levi copied the other man's stance and leaned against the opposite file cabinet, one foot against the door, his thumbs in his jeans pockets.

He needed to get out of here, find Harper and do what he could to fix this. He knew he'd be charged. No idea what the charges would be, but they'd tie him up for a while. Getting to Harper before that happened was more important to him than anything else. Whatever this guy was playing at would have to wait.

Levi straightened up at the same time the stranger spoke. "I ought to kill you."

Well, that was enough to get a guy's attention. "Odd, considering I don't know you, though I assume you have your reasons. You'll have to wait, though. I never kill someone in self-defense before noon. Just a preference, and one my attorney, whom I'm waiting on, wholly approves of."

Levi reached for the door handle, but the agent's response froze him in place as effectively as if he'd been dumped butt naked in the Arctic in January.

"My name's Daniel Miller. I'm Harper's partner."

Levi stepped toward the man. "Where is she? Can I see her?"

"You don't deserve her, you ignorant bastard." He pulled out a pack of gum but didn't offer Levi a piece. Slowly unwrapping it, he folded the stick into his mouth. "You realize she loves you, right?"

He stared at the door, his mind sluggish. "She arrested me." Of course, she'd told him she would if he lied to her. And he had. So she had. But it still stung.

"When?" Daniel asked, the question short and sharp. "Because according to what she told a roomful of federal agents, you're free to go." The man took a step forward.

"As soon as I'm done with you. Small caveat, but whatever."

Levi's feet moved as though they were cased in the mafia's finest cement boots as he shuffled to face Daniel. "Free to go?" he croaked.

Daniel moved in close, his entire body radiating fury. "That woman stood up in front of the FBI, the ATF, her boss and a couple of IRS peers and told them we had no evidence to charge you. And that you, apparently, volunteered to help fill in the holes on the case with your mighty intelligence and familiarity with the legitimate business as you knew it, not as the drug distribution and money-laundering center it is. Or was." Daniel cracked his gum. "Oh, yeah. And then she admitted to breaking the rules and quit."

Light-headed, Levi slid down the door and connected with ground. Hard. "She quit?"

He looked up and caught the brief flash of compassion on the agent's face as the guy kicked a wastebasket closer to him. "If you're going to puke, do it in there."

If Levi looked half as sick as he felt, he understood Daniel's concern. That didn't matter, though. At this point, he cared about only one thing. "Is she okay?"

Daniel considered him for a moment before answering. "Not going to ask me about the club?"

Blinded by a crush of emotions, he surged to his feet, grabbed Daniel by the front of the shirt and drove him into a wide metal file cabinet. The crash would likely draw attention. Levi didn't care. Not about that. Not about getting in a federal agent's face. "Is she okay?" he rasped.

The guy didn't react, but the four words that came out of his mouth nearly laid Levi out. "Do you love her?"

He let go of Daniel's shirt and stepped back, blinking rapidly. "How could I not?"

Daniel grinned, his entire demeanor relaxing. "Right answer, my man."

"Where is she?" He didn't care if it sounded like he was begging. If that's what it took, he'd go to his knees, prostrate himself, call the guy the king of Cheez Whiz if it fulfilled some secret desire of his and would get him to give up information that would bring Levi to Harper faster.

Glancing at his watch, Daniel winced. "She left more than an hour ago. I'm going to bet she's on a plane home to DC." He stared at Levi, his gaze shrewd. "You want her back?"

"Not really. I mean, you love a woman and you lose her, you just replace her, right?" Levi bit out, disregarding the way Daniel tensed up. "Of course I want her back, you jackass!"

Daniel's smile was slower this time, more calculated. "What are you willing to do about it?"

"I'll move heaven and earth." He grabbed his head and squeezed, trying to make his brain override his heart so he could come up with a logical plan. "Whatever it takes."

"Again, right answer." The agent strode toward the door and, opening it, looked back at Levi. He jerked his head toward the hallway. "What're you waiting for, an engraved invitation from Cupid? Get your ass in gear, man. Let's go."

Levi moved without thinking, rushing into the hallway. "You going to help me?"

"No," Daniel said softly. "I'm going to help her."

That was fine. The guy's motivations didn't matter, not if it meant Levi recovered what he'd come so close to losing. He wouldn't accept that it might already be lost. That simply wasn't an option.

Harper might have initially seen him as nothing more than a pretty playboy, but she was wrong.

When it came to getting what he wanted and, where she was concerned, what he needed, Harper Banks was about to learn exactly how ruthless Levi could be.

20

Being home, in her old room where the walls were still decorated with flotsam from childhood, afforded Harper more comfort than she would have guessed. The result? She slept through the first week she was there. When she finally emerged with the intent of rejoining the living, the house was quiet.

She wandered downstairs, well rested but essentially numb. The emotional black hole that had taken up residence in her chest seemed intent on sucking the life right out of her. Every time she started to think about something that hurt, she shoved the thought, the memory, the loneliness into that gaping void.

Better that way, and you know it.

"That you, baby?"

She managed a smile. "Depends," she called back to her dad. "Who you callin' baby besides Mom?"

His deep chuckle left her craving the sight of him.

She took the last few steps two at a time and emerged off the kitchen, pushing through the old swinging door to find her dad seated at the small dining table. Pouring herself a cup of coffee, she pulled up a chair next to him and sipped the worst brew in the world with a shudder. "You still can't make coffee."

"Didn't stop you from drinking it." He grinned. "Never did." Chucking her under the chin, he considered her. "You slept for a week and still look like hell. Your mom's worried." Dadspeak for *he* was worried.

"Why don't you ever own your feelings?" The question was out before she could stop herself.

"Mind your tone," he answered gruffly. "I did. I do." Setting his coffee cup down, the man who'd never aged as she grew seemed older now, with more gray peppering his hair and deeper lines chasing across his face. He picked up a motorcycle magazine.

"Sorry." Twenty-two years melted away in a blink. She was eight again and apologizing to her dad for some variance he disapproved of or a comment he hadn't liked or, heaven help them all should it differ from his, *her opinion.* Pushing away from the table, she abandoned her coffee and started for the swinging door. She'd go back to sleep and try again next week.

"Sit down."

The man's command stopped her, as always. She didn't turn around. "I'm going to bed."

"No, Harper, you're not." His chair legs scraped across the worn linoleum.

She listened to his approach, every step resonating despite the fact his heavy steps were muffled by the thick rubber soles on his trademark boots. The sound made her feel smaller than a field mouse and, for the first time in her life, angry her own father reduced her to that.

Rounding on him, she frowned to find his arms open. "What?"

Discomfort colored his face a strange puce as he dropped his arms. "Far as I know, this is how people hug each other."

A fast-moving river of confusion carried every grain of anger away. *Say something*, her mind commanded. Her mouth made no move to obey when her mind failed to fill the awkward silence.

Her old man frowned. "What?"

"You're going to *hug* me?" she blurted. "You *never* hug me. Why now?"

His frown deepened, making the observed lines look more like emotional fault lines than simple age. "Yeah, I do. Hug you, that is."

"When?" She couldn't stop herself from challenging him.

The color in his face deepened. "Not often enough, according to your mother."

"So she told you to hug me when I got up?" That made more sense. He hadn't changed, hadn't learned from his mistakes. He was only following orders.

"No."

Harper's brow furrowed.

"Not when you got up." Twisting, her dad tossed the magazine he still held. It landed on the table with a distinctive *fwap*, the sound loud in the strange silence between them. "Woman's been harping on me about it all your damn life. Told her you weren't that kind of kid, but she's always been determined I was wrong about that."

"I *am* that kind of kid," she said, voice cracking. "You were just never that kind of father."

His head jerked back as if she'd struck him. "A lifetime of you bein' one way and suddenly you want me to hug you? That's always been your mom's gig. Not mine. I couldn't run around the shop hugging and praising you."

"I was, and am, the child you made me, Dad." Chest tight, Harper fought to keep her voice neutral.

His eyes narrowed. "It was a shop environment. You wanted to be one of the guys, Harper. Always did. Did you see me running around hugging them, praising them for a job well done? It was a business, a hard business with hard men, not some emotional support group urging people to follow their dreams."

"I was your daughter, not a work-hardened fabricator or world-hardened biker," she whispered, and suddenly that wasn't enough. Not anymore. Years of pent-up anger exploded from her with so much anguish a blind man would have wept to hear it. "I was your little girl!" she shouted. "I picked up that rag to polish the tailpipes of that ' 72 FLH Shovelhead Hardtail because I'd seen you do it. I wanted to be what you wanted, even needed, me to be, so I mimicked you."

He stared at her, eyes wide, lips parted.

"What?" she whispered, voice shredded. "You think I'd forget the bike that made me a part of your dream? Or, more importantly, finally a part of your life?"

"You think I wanted you around because you helped in the shop?" he asked so quietly she was forced to focus to hear him over the hum of the refrigerator.

"You always said never settle for good enough if you can be better. So I followed that rule until it became habit— a habit you liked, which made me more determined than ever to stick to what became the golden rule."

He winced, opened his mouth then closed it, his lips disappearing into a thin line. His chin dipped to his chest as a slight shiver passed over him.

"Dad?"

When he looked up, his eyes were bright. "I've done you a lifetime of wrong, baby girl."

Panic bit at her, bloodying what little remained of her self-confidence. "No, I didn't mean—"

"Hush. *Hush*," he said when she tried to speak. "I'm going to say this once, and you need to hear it." His gaze skipped around the room as if picking up different ideas from random, inanimate objects—false fruit, faded lace curtains, the coffee machine, the stove top. When he finally spoke, his gravelly voice was tight enough that, had it been a tightrope, it would have supported an elephant. "I never knew what to do with you before you started coming to the shop. You were this fearless, charming, adorable, *feminine* girl. You shadowed your mother and had little interest in me. Then, when you were four, you picked up a shop rag and went to work."

His voice thickened. "You wanted to be one of the guys so bad, so I treated you that way. You ate it up. And so did I. You suddenly wanted *me*, not your mother. You asked *me* to tuck you into bed. You asked *me* to come to your softball games. You asked *me* to take you to college. You wanted *me*." His voice cracked. "And I didn't ever want that to change. Even when things started falling apart at the shop, I couldn't let you go, and so I dragged you down with me."

Her heartache defied the black hole in her chest, returning with a vengeance. "It was my failure, too, Dad."

"No, my failure was giving up. Something you never did. After the shop closed, you threw yourself into the business with Marcus. And after that…ended, you became the best IRS investigator in your division. You're so much stronger than me, Harper. Don't let fear keep you from the things you love." He finally looked up, and his eyes were bright. "And I love you. From day one, you were my baby girl. Always," he said fiercely.

"You never told me."

"My biggest regret."

"More than losing the shop?"

"The shop mattered, Harper. Don't ever think it didn't. But I survived losing it. Losing you? I wouldn't survive that."

The first sob tore from her throat as he closed the distance and wrapped her in his embrace. He held her as she shook, whispering to her about the levels of his love, how deep it ran and how unchanging it would always be.

When her sobs quieted, she made to move out of his embrace.

He tightened his grip. "Now tell me who else broke your heart."

"Marcus—"

"You never loved him, Harp. You wanted to love him, but that's nowhere near the same. This? You quitting your job and spending a week sleeping to ward off the hurt?" He leaned back then and met her gaze. "This is love."

"I think I blew it," she choked out.

"What did I just say? Love is a lot harder to destroy than you credit it with. Now go be the fearless woman I know you are."

"I love you, Dad." The unfamiliar words tripped off her tongue.

"Almost as much as I love you," he replied softly, taking her hand and leading her back to the table. "Now stop avoiding the question. You're not a federal agent anymore, so who do I need to kill?"

LEVI STOOD ON the saltbox house's shallow porch, one fist planted on the door frame. The other fist had been raised to knock for several minutes. His follow-through sucked.

It had taken him two months to wrap up helping the IRS, and another full week to track Harper down in DC. He'd been there yesterday only to find the house she owned empty, a For Sale sign parked at the curb. He'd called Daniel, made a lot of promises while Daniel made several threats, but finally the guy told Levi where Harper had gone. Stunned, he'd caught a cab back to the airport and bought a ticket to the closest airport to Nashville. One stay in a hotel, a car rental and a three-hour drive had delivered him to her parents' doorstep in Bell Buckle, Tennessee. That's where his nerve had abandoned him.

Fighting the urge to sit in the car and wait for her to come out so he could just see her and get his bearings before facing her again, he forced himself to knock. Seconds later, Grizzly Adams opened the door. Levi stared at the man—tall enough to stare him eye to eye but with a good fifty pounds of beer belly giving him the weight advantage—who could only be Harper's father.

"You better be here for the right reasons, boy, or you're in for a world of hurt," the behemoth rumbled, moving out on the porch.

Levi stepped back, but only far enough to allow the man room to pull the door shut behind him. "You clearly know who I am."

One bushy eyebrow arched. "Clearly."

"I need to see Harper, Mr. Banks."

"Why?"

The question, full of challenge, landed at Levi's feet with an earthshaking rumble. "That's between me and Harper."

He glared at Levi through slitted gray eyes. "Boy, you sent her home to me broken, so you'll either answer my question or I'll drop-kick your assless-chap-wearing, pretty-boy, hippie-haircut, stubborn-as-hell self all the way back to the West Coast."

"You think?" Levi drawled, his temper spiking. He hadn't come all this way to have the door shut in his face. Not by anyone.

"Only because she's forbidden me from huntin' you down, puttin' a bullet between your eyes and leavin' your body to science as proof that assholes can grow legs, walk and talk."

The guy gave good threat…but not good enough to make Levi leave. Banking on his revised approach to life, he did the only thing his conscience would allow. He told the truth. "Threaten me all you'd like, Mr. Banks. No doubt I've earned it. But I love your daughter, and I'm not leaving here until I see her and make sure she knows *exactly* how I feel. If she wants me to leave after she's heard me out, fine. But you better be prepared for me to camp in my car across the road, because I'm not leaving until she understands just how far I'm willing to go to get her back."

The man looked him over silently. Then he dug a set of keys out of his jeans pocket and grinned through his heavy beard. "Handy, then, that I've got something to do in town and she'll be here by herself for, oh, at least two hours." Opening the door, he motioned Levi through while he stayed on the porch. As Levi passed, Banks leaned in and issued his parting advice. "Get this right, boy, because no one hurts my baby girl." Then he leaned his head in the door and shouted, "Harper!"

"Yeah?" she answered.

At the sound of her voice, Levi's heart constricted.

"Get down here, pronto." With a wink, the giant man soundlessly shut and locked the door.

Levi watched Harper descend the stairs. She wore a white T-shirt and navy sweatpants. Her short hair was a mess. Thick socks covered her slender feet.

Had she changed her nail polish or was it still pink?

He shifted his focus to her face, hoping against hope to see even a hint of excitement at finding him in her home. What he found instead were wide eyes that betrayed visible, soul-shattering hurt. No, not hurt. That was far too mild for what he saw reflected in those gray eyes.

Man up and call it what it is, his conscience demanded.

So he did.

It was unbearable heartache.

And he was responsible.

He swallowed at the familiar surge of self-recrimination.

Yes, this was essentially all his fault. He'd spent weeks trying to do the right thing, and Daniel had been forwarding little tidbits to her to ensure she knew where he'd been and what he'd been doing. ˙

But she hadn't reached out, not to him. Not once had she pressed Daniel about him. The only thing she'd said when Daniel asked what she was going to do now was to say she intended to fall off the grid for a bit but she'd be in touch when she resurfaced.

In touch. Resurfaced.

The words had been parked in the center of his chest like a metric ton of terror for weeks. It could be days, weeks, months or more before anyone heard from her, and he wouldn't have a clue where to start looking. Daniel had assured him he could track her down, but Levi had dismissed that idea. Harper had a right to live her life as she chose, even if those choices didn't include him.

You're standing here like a complete fool. Get on with it, already.

His conscience, as he'd recently learned, could be a real ass. Practical, but still an ass.

He cleared his throat, never taking his eyes off her. "Hi."

Harper looked over her shoulder and back up the stairs as she responded. "Now's not really the best time for me."

He shrugged, fighting to remain calm. "I would imagine it's not, but I'm here and I intend to make the most of it."

The life in her eyes seemed to snuff out, and she stepped away. "You don't have any right to do this to me, Levi."

He moved forward another few inches, this time leaning his against the newel post. "What, exactly, have I done?"

"You showed up. Given our history, I consider that more than enough," she said and followed through on the stairs thing, starting back up them with purpose. "Leave."

With no other options clear to him, he reached out and grabbed her arm, spinning her to face him.

"What are you doing?" she asked, her tone flat.

"I want to talk to you."

"Then use the freaking phone like a normal person. Now get out." She yanked her arm free and, changing direction, started through the living room, her stride long and sure, socked feet making hardly a sound on the floor.

"Not happening, Harper." His legs were longer, his desperation far sharper, and he caught her less than halfway across the room. Arms wrapped tightly around her, he hauled her against his body.

If she still wanted him to leave after he'd said his piece, he'd do his best to honor her wishes without being reduced to begging. He figured he had at best a ninety-ten shot of preserving his pride, and the odds weren't in his favor.

Her heart hammered against the arm that crossed her chest, beating against his skin as if it intended to dislodge him and make a mad dash for freedom. He wanted to soothe and reassure her, but he wasn't a fool. If he let her go, she'd come at him like a wounded predator who'd been cornered. The hard part for him was that he'd been the one to both wound her and corner her, but he didn't know what else to do. "Just…hear me out."

"How much more do you think I can take? How much more do *I* have to suffer so you can sleep soundly at night?" The soft hitch in her voice betrayed her rigid body. When his only response was to hold her tighter, she sort of wilted as she let out a shuddering breath. "Say whatever it is you need to say and go. Please. I'm tapped out, Levi. I've got nothing left."

The undisguised despair in her voice cut him.

Deep.

Closing his eyes, he fought to slow his breathing. Everything he'd planned to say, all the right words and tender truths, were suddenly inadequate when compared to the depth of what he felt for the woman who, willing or not, he held in his arms. What he had left to offer her was the only thing she'd ever asked him to promise her—truth, no matter how badly it hurt—so that's what he'd give. "Hear me out. If you still want me to go when I'm done, I'll go."

"Fine."

Much as he wanted to cling to her, he let her go.

She didn't speak to him as she walked through the room and into a bright but aged kitchen. He followed closely, leaning against the counter on one side as she hoisted herself onto the island across from him. She waved her hand, motioning for him to get on with it.

He gave a short nod. Gripping the counter behind him so he'd have something to do with his hands other than touch her, he lifted his chin, blew out a deep breath and set every ounce of pride aside, odds be damned. "Until about ten weeks ago, life was good. I worked the club at night, did trades during the day, made good money, had female companionship when I wanted it and some pretty tight friends. I took every moment for granted like it was my God-given right to want for nothing." His voice wavered, so he paused for a second, fighting for control. "One knock on the door changed everything."

Harper's chin dipped to her chest, her shoulders rolling forward as she scooted toward the island's edge.

"Don't. Run." The command was so viciously raw he didn't even recognize his own voice.

She stopped, closed her eyes and wrapped her arms around her middle as if to cradle herself.

He swallowed around the bitter fear lodged in his throat and continued. "In walks this woman, so sure of herself, intelligent, in control. It didn't hurt she was hot as hell. For the first time, it stung that a woman thought I wasn't worth more than a few bucks after a little bump and grind on the stage. In no way did my bruised pride justify the decisions I made, particularly when I chose to lie to her."

Her chin came up at that. All color had leeched from her face, leaving her skin so pale against the white of her T-shirt that her eyes were dark pools under her brows.

He dug his fingers into the counter even harder, muscles trembling with the effort to hold himself in check. If he let go, he had no doubt he'd throw himself at her. It wouldn't help. He had to finish this. "It was my choice, Harper. I own that. I own every damn lie I laid at your feet. I initially thought I'd done it to protect the people who were, at the time, the most important people in my life."

"I knew you'd lied to me. I gave you several chances to own up."

He let his head fall back and stared at the ceiling. "Yeah." His chin tipped forward. Letting go of the counter, he closed the distance between them, hooked a finger under her chin and lifted her face to his. "What I need *you* to understand is that, even before things escalated between us, I regretted the choices I'd made."

A sad smile lifted one corner of her mouth. "Me, too."

He nodded. "I saw you, really saw you, long before I first kissed you. That kiss, though…" As he absently ran his thumb along her jaw, it destroyed him to watch the first tear tip over her lower lashes and lazily roll down her cheek. "That kiss changed everything. And when you took me to bed at the hotel, then at Cass's apartment? When I had your bare skin under my hands and the sounds of your pleasure filling my head? I was sure, Harper. It was as clear as if someone had spoken in my ear, 'This is the one.'"

She started to shake her head, her denial absolute.

Gently gripping her face in his hands, he leaned forward and kissed her forehead. Then he stepped back and waited for her to look up at him. It felt like hours before she did, but when it finally happened, Levi said what he'd crossed the continent to say. "You listen to me, Harper

Banks. You listen and you hear. You taught me the difference between want and need. I wanted you when I met you, but that night? That's when I truly understood that what I felt for you was so much more than want. I needed you. And in that moment, when my need for you superseded my need for everything and everyone else? That's when I realized I was completely lost to you. Without looking for it, the thing I'd needed most had found me. That was you, Harper. I've fallen hopelessly, unapologetically and insanely in love with you."

21

SHOCK, TERROR, JOY and a handful of accompanying emotions whipped up a tempestuous storm that thundered through Harper without apology. She hadn't realized she had enough of any one emotion left to wreak such havoc. Buffeted by invisible violence, she took strength where she found it, meeting Levi's eyes, wrapping her hands around his wrists and holding on as he cradled her face.

He never looked away, never flinched when her blunt nails dug into his skin.

"I don't know how to do this," she murmured.

"Do what?" he asked quietly.

"Find a place to start over with someone."

He canted her head back a bit to ensure she was staring right at him when he spoke. "It took me a while to realize that it's not really about starting over, sweetheart." His lips found hers, the kiss almost painfully tender. "Besides, I wouldn't even if I could."

"We could save each other so much hurt."

"True, but if we started over, there's a chance we might not end up exactly where we have to be, which is here. Now." A second kiss, firmer this time. "My only regret is that I can't bear your pain for you. I would, Harper.

I'd take it in a heartbeat and never complain. I'm sorry I lied, and living with the knowledge I hurt you so badly is my own personal hell, but I won't apologize for loving you. Not now. Not ever." He dropped his hands and stepped away. "I promised you honesty, always, and that's what you'll get from me. That means I owe you another apology."

The emotional storm that had raged in her went silent. "Excuse me?"

"I told you before that, after I said what I'd come to say, I would leave if you wanted me to. At the time I said it, I intended to keep my word. I've changed my mind." He shrugged and grinned, the look blatantly sexual and totally unapologetic. "Good luck getting rid of me."

"You can't stay here," she blurted out.

"Fine. I'll find a place nearby."

"No."

His face darkened. "Yes."

"No, I mean I'm leaving tomorrow. I'm opening my own shop."

"Then I'll go with you and help. But you are *not* leaving me, sweetheart," he said, the words ringing with intent.

He moved in close, situating himself between her thighs, smiling when she cringed. "You don't like sweetheart? Then we'll come up with something else. Whatever we settle on, I intend to use. It's just one more way to say I love you."

It was the strangest thing. Tenderness moved through her at his aggression, an unexpected balm to her battered heart. "How many ways are there? To say, 'I love you,' I mean."

"I honestly have no idea." His hands slid around her hips to cup her ass, dragging her forward so her sex pressed against the hard ridge of his erection. "I'll make you a deal, though."

Her arms snaked around his neck as the knowledge that this, this thing with him, was absolutely right. She'd been sure the night she'd lain in his arms that Levi was everything she'd wanted Marcus to be and so much more. And she'd been sure later that same day at Seattle's federal building that she'd had a chance to set things right with Levi, to love him the way he was meant to be loved—wholly, completely, thoroughly, daily—but she'd run. She was done running. She was going to face this with bravery. No, not even bravery. She would be fearless in everything that involved this amazing man.

Wrapping her legs around his waist, she leaned in to nuzzle his neck. "What's your deal, Walsh?"

"Spend your life with me and I'll do my best to find a new way to tell you I love you every day."

"And if I decline?"

He went still. "Doesn't really matter. I'll spend *my* life doing whatever I have to do to convince you to come over to my way of thinking."

"That's my man," she said, nipping his earlobe.

"Is that a yes?" he asked, the question infused with a hunger she prayed time would never dull.

"That's a yes."

He drove his hands though her hair and hauled her head back, closing his mouth over hers and demanding entrance. The kiss evolved into a kind of desperate reclaiming they both needed. Breaking away, eyes slightly wild, he tightened his grip on her hair. "Say it. Put me out of my misery."

She didn't have to ask. Like spoke to like, heart to heart, and she knew what he wanted. More, she knew what he needed. "I love you, Levi Walsh."

He closed his eyes. Voice rough, he said, "I swear you'll never regret it."

There was no doubt in her mind that he was telling her the absolute truth.

* * * * *

REQUEST YOUR FREE BOOKS!
2 FREE NOVELS PLUS 2 FREE GIFTS!

HARLEQUIN®

Blaze®

red-hot reads!

YES! Please send me 2 FREE Harlequin® Blaze™ novels and my 2 FREE gifts (gifts are worth about $10). After receiving them, if I don't wish to receive any more books, I can return the shipping statement marked "cancel." If I don't cancel, I will receive 4 brand-new novels every month and be billed just $4.74 per book in the U.S. or $4.96 per book in Canada. That's a savings of at least 14% off the cover price. It's quite a bargain. Shipping and handling is just 50¢ per book in the U.S. and 75¢ per book in Canada.* I understand that accepting the 2 free books and gifts places me under no obligation to buy anything. I can always return a shipment and cancel at any time. Even if I never buy another book, the two free books and gifts are mine to keep forever.

150/350 HDN F4WC

Name _____ (PLEASE PRINT)

Address _____ Apt. #

City _____ State/Prov. _____ Zip/Postal Code

Signature (if under 18, a parent or guardian must sign)

Mail to the **Harlequin® Reader Service:**
IN U.S.A.: P.O. Box 1867, Buffalo, NY 14240-1867
IN CANADA: P.O. Box 609, Fort Erie, Ontario L2A 5X3

Want to try two free books from another line?
Call 1-800-873-8635 or visit www.ReaderService.com.

* Terms and prices subject to change without notice. Prices do not include applicable taxes. Sales tax applicable in N.Y. Canadian residents will be charged applicable taxes. Offer not valid in Quebec. This offer is limited to one order per household. Not valid for current subscribers to Harlequin Blaze books. All orders subject to credit approval. Credit or debit balances in a customer's account(s) may be offset by any other outstanding balance owed by or to the customer. Please allow 4 to 6 weeks for delivery. Offer available while quantities last.

Your Privacy—The Harlequin® Reader Service is committed to protecting your privacy. Our Privacy Policy is available online at www.ReaderService.com or upon request from the Harlequin Reader Service.

We make a portion of our mailing list available to reputable third parties that offer products we believe may interest you. If you prefer that we not exchange your name with third parties, or if you wish to clarify or modify your communication preferences, please visit us at www.ReaderService.com/consumerschoice or write to us at Harlequin Reader Service Preference Service, P.O. Box 9062, Buffalo, NY 14269. Include your complete name and address.

HB13R2

SPECIAL EXCERPT FROM

HARLEQUIN®

Blaze

*Military veteran Mia Brandt agrees to a fake
engagement to help sexy rescue swimmer Tag Johnson
out of a jam. But could their fun, temporary liaison lead
to something more?*

Read on for a sneak preview at
WICKED SECRETS *by* **Anne Marsh**,
part of our **UNIFORMLY HOT!** *miniseries.*

Sailor boy didn't look up. Not because he didn't notice
the other woman's departure—something about the way
he held himself warned her he was aware of everyone
and everything around him—but because polite clearly
wasn't part of his daily repertoire.

Fine. She wasn't all that civilized herself.

The blonde made a face, her ponytail bobbing as she
started hoofing it along the beach. "Good luck with that
one," she muttered as she passed Mia.

Oookay. Maybe this *was* mission impossible. Still,
she'd never failed when she'd been out in the field, and
all her gals wanted was intel. She padded into the water,
grateful for the cool soaking into her burning soles. The
little things mattered so much more now.

"I'm not interested." Sailor boy didn't look up from
the motor when she approached, a look of fierce concen-
tration creasing his forehead. Having worked on more
than one Apache helicopter during her two tours of duty,
she knew the repair work wasn't rocket science.

She also knew the mechanic and…holy hotness.

Mentally, she ran through every curse word she'd learned. Tag Johnson hadn't changed much in five years. He'd acquired a few more fine lines around the corners of his eyes, possibly from laughing. Or from squinting into the sun since rescue swimmers spent plenty of time out at sea. The white scar on his forearm was as new as the lines, but otherwise he was just as gorgeous and every bit as annoying as he'd been the night she'd picked him up at the Star Bar in San Diego. He was also still out of her league, a military bad boy who was strong, silent, deadly…and always headed out the door.

For a brief second, she considered retreating. Unfortunately, the bridal party was watching her intently, clearly hoping she was about to score on their behalf. Disappointing them would be a shame.

"Funny," she drawled. "You could have fooled me."

Tag's head turned slowly toward her. Mia had hoped for drama. Possibly even his butt planting in the ocean from the surprise of her reappearance. No such luck.

"Sergeant Dominatrix," he drawled back.

Don't miss
WICKED SECRETS
by New York Times *bestselling author Anne Marsh,*
available April 2015 wherever
Harlequin® Blaze® books and ebooks are sold.

www.Harlequin.com

JUST CAN'T GET ENOUGH?

Join our social communities
and talk to us online.

You will have access to the latest
news on upcoming titles and special
promotions, but most importantly,
you can talk to other fans about your
favorite Harlequin reads.

Harlequin.com/Community

Facebook.com/HarlequinBooks

Twitter.com/HarlequinBooks

Pinterest.com/HarlequinBooks

HARLEQUIN®

A Romance FOR EVERY MOOD™

Stay up-to-date on all your
romance-reading news with the
Harlequin Shopping Guide,
featuring bestselling authors, exciting new
miniseries, books to watch and more!

The newest issue will be delivered right to you
with our compliments! There are 4 each year.

Signing up is easy.

EMAIL

ShoppingGuide@Harlequin.ca

WRITE TO US

HARLEQUIN BOOKS
Attention: Customer Service Department
P.O. Box 9057, Buffalo, NY 14269-9057

OR PHONE

1-800-873-8635 in the United States
1-888-343-9777 in Canada

Please allow 4-6 weeks for delivery of the first issue by mail.